THE TEN ARMS OF DURGA

A SONYA KELLER ADVENTURE

Mirador Publishing
10 Greenbrook Terrace
Taunton
Somerset
UK
TA1 1UT

The Ten Arms of Durga

A Sonya Keller Adventure

By

Vern Turner

Contents

Preface

WHO OR WHAT IS "DURGA"? For a long time, while writing this story, I struggled with finding a title. Nothing seemed to work. One day I searched for angels of justice or goddesses of the oppressed, and up popped the Vishnu consort Durga.

The legends have it that Durga was empowered by the Hindu gods to defend the innocent against demons and other evil characters. The legends also describe her as having anywhere from four to ten arms. In each of those arms and hands, the gods placed a different weapon for Durga to sally forth and, literally, slay the dragons afflicting the innocent.

The character I created here may push the boundaries of plausibility from time to time, but I had to harken back to eras gone by where some athletes were SO much better than their peers at the time that in today's parlance, they would be called superstars.

I went to college with an astonishing track star. He ran world-class times from 100 meters to a mile, or 1,500 meters. He just missed qualifying for the 800 meters at the 1964 Olympic trials. That example gave this author some actual credence to developing the incredible performance by the main character. Add to that, Mildred "Babe" Didrikson was an astonishing athlete during the 1930s and 40s. She was heptathlete strong, an Olympics champion and picked up very complex games like golf quickly such that she started winning every tournament she entered. George Herman "Babe" Ruth was another athlete who stood, literally, head and shoulders above his contemporaries setting baseball records thought unbreakable. Mike Powell broke the long jump record by almost 2 feet in 1991. He never repeated that feat again.

As you'll soon see, Sonya Keller's superior athleticism, combined with her other skill sets and an unquenchable drive to "defend the innocent" make us all not only realize our own limitations and mortality, but how certain events in concert with a highly unusual genetic package can create beings and moments of wonder.

This story begins a series involving Sonya Keller and the circumstances she encounters and overcomes in various settings in modern day America. Some of those experiences are tragic. Some are truly heroic, and more still push the limits of human endurance.

Gastonburg, Indiana is fictitious. Muncie, Indiana, Gary, Indiana, Chicago, Illinois and Ball State University are real. All characters, unless otherwise noted, are totally fictitious and any resemblance to real people is purely coincidental.

Chapter 1

THE VIOLATION

THE TWELVE-YEAR-OLD GIRL purposefully pushed her father's hands away as he drunkenly began groping her. Sonya was a bit more developed than most girls her age, and since she entered puberty, her father had started making lewd comments, pulling her onto his lap, and constantly tried pawing her body, especially when he was drinking. The stench of stale alcohol on his breath was enough to make her nauseous and yearn to be away from him. The love she may have felt for her father dissipated more with each episode of his obvious desire to fondle her body. She knew she was no longer "daddy's little girl", and at times like this, she didn't even want to be his girl in any way.

The girl's father, Cromwell (Crummy) Keller, grew up charming people with his magnetic personality, matinee idol good looks and athletic body. He managed to induce a former homecoming queen, Erica Moorhead to marry him when he turned twenty and she was just eighteen.

Erica Moorhead was tall, athletic and, by most modern American standards, considered beautiful. She had light brown hair, captivating blue eyes and deep dimples on each side of her dazzling smile. She came from a traditional, blue-collar, working-man's family. Her father, Jonah was a machinist at a local factory. He was tall, muscular, ruggedly handsome and remarkably ignorant of anything outside of his work and his lust for alcohol. Her mother, Mildred, adhered to the traditional housewife's role. Mildred was also tall, but lanky. She once had a pretty face that was now lined and drawn from the years of child-rearing and fending off the drunken rages from her husband. The constant smoking of cigarettes helped to line her face, roughen her voice and advance the aging process such that she looked years older than she was. In sum, she appeared to be a person who only knew unhappiness.

ERICA'S TWO OLDER BROTHERS, SETH and Morris, escaped into the military right after their eighteenth birthdays. They both played high school football, were very ordinary students in school, and basically ignored Erica leaving her to feel like an only child. They were handsome boys as their parentage would demand, but they both displayed a kind of vapidness that made one wonder whether they were aware of their surroundings or not.

Jonah was a strict parent who, as most blue-collar workers in the rust belt did, drank heavily and often fell asleep with his clothes on. He interacted rarely with Erica. She was just a girl, after all. Jonah was thrilled when she got married and moved out of the house. He saw it as one less mouth to feed and made sure Erica knew his attitude on the subject. There simply was very little love or kindness in the Moorhead house, and the dour, unsmiling countenance of everyone involved reflected that atmosphere to the world.

Cromwell Keller was also tall, athletic and good-looking. He was raised on the other side of town from Erica, and his parents, Steven and Bernice, were both professionals working in the banking industry. His high school pals accepted the "Crummy" nickname for him from an opposing baseball team after they lost badly while he tried pitching his school team into their district's playoffs.

Crummy had two older sisters, Maggie and Alice. The Keller sisters were considered pretty by those who knew them. Popularity in high school was not their biggest problem as they were rather promiscuous; avoiding pregnancy was their major field of interest while doing their best to defeat that process. Maggie and Alice were a little taller than medium height but displayed buxomness from their earliest days of puberty. The boys at school followed them around like puppies chasing rubber balls...which, in a sense, was rather accurate.

Both sisters teased Crummy mercilessly and played embarrassing and often vicious tricks on him from his earliest memories until they went to college in subsequent years. The girls found it especially joy-inducing to sprinkle Crummy's undershorts with finely ground red pepper. Tying the laces of his favorite basketball shoes together and then throwing them over power lines invoked rage from Crummy much to their delight.

At age sixteen, and free of his sisters' harassment, Crummy went to work part-time at a local appliance repair shop. He was a quick learner and the owner took him under his wing to teach him the mechanics of things ranging from refrigerators to air-conditioners. By the time he graduated high school, he was an expert at the craft of large – and small - appliance repair.

During his junior year in high school, Crummy Keller met Erica Moorhead while she was waiting tables at an ice cream shop not far from Erica's high school. Crummy's football team had arrived early to eat their pre-game meal that particular night. Erica was overwhelmed by Crummy's good looks and physique. Crummy, of course, was dazzled by Erica's natural beauty and alluring figure – exaggerated by her short, tight skirt that exposed shapely, nicely toned legs. Crummy asked for and received her phone number and they began dating regularly. Their relationship became increasingly intimate, but Erica managed to avoid getting pregnant and creating the obligatory scandal for herself. She thought that her father would certainly kick her out of the house if she became "in the club".

At age twenty, before Crummy and Erica married, an air-conditioning company recruited him to be an applications engineer. This meant he would evaluate a potential customer's appliance or heating/air-conditioning (HVAC) needs and design the right system to satisfy them. After he settled into that job, he felt secure enough to finally set a wedding date with his beautiful fiancée, Erica Moorhead. They embarked on a storybook marriage by doing everything differently than either sets of parents did in their day-to-day activities. They made it a point to share everything with each other and do things they both enjoyed. Erica kept waiting tables to earn a little more money, but "graduated" from the ice cream parlor to an up-scale restaurant. Her looks and charm yielded good tips from customers and beaming approval from her manager.

Sonya Keller appeared in Erica's and Crummy's life about a year after they were married filling them with joy. Sonya was a wonderfully cute child with a sweet disposition, fetching dimples, wavy, light-brown hair and big, blue eyes the color of robin's eggs. She was also quite long of body when born and continued to defy the child development charts as she grew. By the time she turned twelve, she was nearly 5 feet, 6 inches tall and towered over her school mates in sixth grade, while accepting all the taunts and teases with an air of diffidence. Budding breasts and gangly limbs did little to disguise the growing beauty and athleticism of this pre-adolescent girl.

After a few years of successfully developing his application engineering skills, Crummy was awarded his own sales position with a good territory surrounding Gastonburg.

It was after Sonya's birth that Crummy Keller started drinking more dark whiskey. His looks started to wane, his wrinkles deepened, and his muscles slackened. His job, selling air-conditioning systems, became more difficult for him as his dependence on alcohol increased. As Erica spent more time with Sonya, Crummy tried to drown his apparent unrequited narcissism in whiskey.

When Sonya was just ten years old, Crummy closed a major deal with a client, Eddie Stemkowski, who offered to share a couple lines of cocaine with him as a celebration for several HVAC units placed in his stores. The client managed a small chain of cheap furniture stores around their town of Gastonburg just outside Gary. He sold furniture to the blue-collar steel and machine shop workers in and around Gastonburg and made a comfortable living. The sale of the new HVAC systems for all of Stemkowski's stores netted Crummy a handsome bonus and commission. So, he thought, a little splurging on a new drug was in order. The client hooked Crummy up with his cocaine supplier, with whom he regularly transacted, to supply Crummy with a fair amount of "weight" to keep him interested.

Crummy devoured the cocaine powder as if he were a Hoover vacuum cleaner. Addiction became too kind a word for what afflicted Crummy. He started going through several hundred dollars' worth of the drug every month. He even invited the dealer over to his house so he could meet Erica and Sonya. It was clear that the dealer, a long-haired, denim-clad, lanky predator-looking man, had his eye on Sonya even though she was just over twelve years old. His name was Raymond ("Just call me Ray") Beddell. His hawk-like eyes were sharp and constantly in motion. He indulged just a smidgen of his own product just to keep Crummy on the hook. Erica could barely stand Ray's presence in her house and asked Crummy to not bring him over anymore. "I don't like the way he looks at Sonya."

"I'll bring any of my friends over who I want. If you don't like it, go out with your dorky pals when he comes over."

"I'm worried that you're spending too much money on booze and dope. I pay the bills and it keeps getting harder every month. Can you cut back on the coke and the booze?"

"Hey! If you're so worried about money, why don't you get off your fat ass and find a job? It's my money we're living on, and I'll do with it what I want. We have enough money to buy food, don't we?"

"Okay. Maybe you're right. I'll look for a job. Sonya is old enough that she could latchkey okay."

"Right. You do that." This decision removed a layer of protection from Sonya so that when she came home from school, only her father and often some of his low-life pals were there.

With that conversation over, Crummy poured himself another three fingers of bourbon and settled down to watch the Pacers play basketball on TV. This particular argument would not be their last over Crummy's new enthrallment with cocaine. As with most addictions, the deterioration of Crummy's personality and behavior increased. Erica's and Crummy's arguments increased covering more topics and with elevated intensity. Sonya would cringe in her bedroom as the voices rose and arguments raged. She often cried herself to sleep as she feared for her own welfare as well as that of her mother. She and her mother had bonded years ago and were more like sisters than mother and daughter. It caused her great, searing pain to see her mother in tears as the verbal abuse from Crummy increased. Something had to change, she felt, but had no idea what to do. Even though their home was modest, Erica intended to keep her "nest" so that her beautiful daughter would keep feeling secure and loved. Those hopes soon became a pipe dream...so to speak.

Meanwhile, Sonya continued to grow. She passed 5 feet 9 inches on her thirteenth birthday. She liked school, and despite the constant harassment of the very immature and mindless teenage boys, she excelled in class and was a favorite among her teachers and female classmates. Most subjects came easy for her, but her gym classes were her favorite. She found she could dominate all the other girls in team sports. She could run faster than they could and was always picked to be the center of the basketball teams because of her height.

One day, just after her fourteenth birthday, Sonya came home from school to find her house filled with men of various ages and in various forms of working-class clothes. Her mother had not yet come home from work. The smell of marijuana was overwhelming, beer bottles were strewn everywhere and there were razor blades and rolled dollar bills all over the coffee table. As she came through the front door, all conversation stopped, and she felt the eyes of the men undressing her from top to bottom. She scurried into her room to the sound of whistles and rude remarks. Her father's cackling laugh could be heard among the hoots.

Sonya kept growing after her thirteenth birthday and was now nearing 6 feet in height. Her body proportions remained balanced and she didn't have the physical awkwardness that often comes with a young woman's emergence into adulthood. She had let her hair grow long so that it was now just at her waist. She had lost all the pre-adolescent cuteness, and the boys at school continued to pester her and followed her everywhere. As their subtle harassment became increasingly rude, she felt ill-prepared and very dis-inclined to be social with them. This problem had the ripple effect of driving her personality inward and making her less socially inclined with everyone. Sonya continued liking school, though, and did her homework diligently, learning as much as she could. She even enjoyed history and science. Her grades were above average, and she participated in the school choir. Her teachers liked her and sent glowing reports home that pleased her mother greatly. Some teachers even hinted that Sonya should be considered for gifted and talented programs.

Meanwhile, it remained a miracle that her father still had a job in view of his taking more and more time away from it to do just what he was doing today. He said that his job was boring and that getting high was an escape for him. He also forced his hugs and kisses on Sonya whenever possible, and she became quite good at squirming out of his drunken grasps. When Erica was home, Crummy kept his hands to himself. A sort of truce developed between Crummy and Erica, and their earlier affections became more perfunctory as the months wore on. Clearly, life in the Keller household deteriorated as everyone in that house just kept their heads down and plowed along one day at a time. Only Crummy seemed somewhat elevated as he stayed high for as many hours per day as he could, thus exacerbating the domestic decay.

Crummy was finally fired from his job after too many binge-induced absences and customer complaints. Erica had found work with a law firm as a kind of go-fer but continued to work her way up the firm's employment ladder. The Kellers were now in a serious financial bind with Erica's salary, now as an executive secretary in the law firm, being barely enough to cover the mortgage and a greatly reduced grocery list. Erica's good looks and emerging office skills impressed the law partners and she moved up the ladder fairly quickly, but her salary didn't allow them to have any luxuries or put away any savings. Crummy, however, remained addicted to drugs, but now a new, less expensive chemical found its way into his rapidly deteriorating brain tissue: *methamphetamine.* Not only did it make Crummy think he was higher than ever, it accelerated his irrational behavior. And Ray Beddell was happy to add this product to Crummy's regular supplies of weed and coke. Beddell became a regular visitor to the Keller home and terrified Sonya with his smirking, leering, side-long glances in her direction. He reminded her of a predatory fox in a dark cartoon.

Erica finally became a victim of domestic violence. One night, after she scurried to her room, locking the door, Sonya heard her parents yelling and arguing like never before. A loud *smack* was followed by a resonant *thump.* Sonya threw open her bedroom door and ran down the hall to the main part of the house where she saw her mother dragging herself to her feet with blood streaming in rivers from her mouth and nose. Standing over her mother was her father with fists clenched.

"Don't you ever try to tell me what to do! It's because of you that I got fired. You wouldn't support me. You shoot your fucking mouth off to me again and I'll send those pretty white teeth down your throat! You hear me?"

Sonya ran to her mother and helped her up. She sat her down in a chair and ran to the kitchen to retrieve a wet towel. Just as she was returning, her father grabbed her by her long hair and pulled her face right up to his own. "As for you, you damned leech, I'm going to teach you some lessons too. We've been way too easy on you and now you're going to learn what it's like to obey the man of the house."

With that, he threw Sonya at her mother where she tumbled over the chair and landed in a heap. She picked herself up and started to sop up the blood from her stunned mother's face. Sonya's hands trembled as she tried to clean the blood off Erica's face. Erica seemed to snap out of a trance and pushed Sonya's hand away. "I'm all right. I can clean myself up. Go back to your room. Lock the door."

Sonya did as she was told. It was the first time she felt utterly helpless and terrified. She was a *good* girl. Why did her father hit her mother and scream at her? Did she do something wrong? Sonya curled up in the corner of her room and cried herself to sleep. She was only fifteen and the ugliness and violence her father showed her shook Sonya to her core. She didn't exactly know what to do next, but she knew that her time in this house was coming to an end.

The tension in the Keller household was like an over-tuned guitar string. There were no apologies from Crummy, nor any changes in his attitude. If anything, Crummy became more wicked and his temper shortened. Erica was clearly frightened to the point of staying in a catatonic state. She couldn't get out of the house fast enough in the mornings and she did everything she could to make a dinner and disappear into her room in the evenings. Sleeping in the same bed as Crummy was out of the question no matter how hard he tried to have sex with her. He was usually so wasted that he couldn't function anyway. The times when he was "alive" enough, he basically forced himself on her in what an outsider would call marriage rape. There were many nights when Erica shared a bed in Sonya's room and cried herself to sleep while her teen-aged daughter tried to console her.

Sonya tried to avoid Crummy and his pals whenever she could, but sometimes Crummy would grab her as she came home from school and embarrass her in front of his friends. They all laughed at her discomfort and her powerlessness to resist. Soon, she just stopped struggling, let him have his fun and then bolted to the shower to wash the stench and the humiliation off as best she could.

Sonya told her mother what was happening, but Erica felt helpless to do anything lest she get another beating. As with most battered women, she wore long-sleeved tops and had over-sized sunglasses that she wore along with thick make-up while the bruises on her face healed. Sonya and Erica traced the changes in healing colors from purple to green to yellow. She was constantly making new excuses at work, but it was clear to everyone what was happening. Both women were becoming increasingly depressed and fearful. Sonya shied away from all adult men to the point of even crossing the street if one was walking toward her. The tightness in her stomach was becoming constant from the time she awoke until sleep blissfully captured her consciousness. Erica's parents had long since disowned her because of Crummy's erratic behavior and open insults to them. She had tried to tell them of the abuse she was receiving from Crummy, but they copped out by condemning her with "she had made her own bed and now had to lie in it." What these ignorant people couldn't imagine was the monster that their daughter's husband had become. His escalating drug habits were in line with Erica's father's alcoholism, so they were immune to seeing the abuse as anything but normal. Erica felt trapped and felt her humanity being stripped away on a daily basis. She felt she was losing her mind, her pride and her soul. Her body hurt somewhere most of the time. She couldn't do anything to prevent Sonya from being abused either, and that added to her misery. When she did protest, she received another beating. The worst was yet to come.

Meanwhile, Sonya made a friend at school named Kelsey Morrow. Kelsey was a dark-skinned, African-American girl of medium height, but with well-defined muscles wherever she allowed them to show. She and Sonya were able to laugh and study together. Sonya was just turning sixteen and learning to play basketball better as her body grew. Kelsey was a very good athlete and helped Sonya develop her skills. The girls came to respect and love each other as sisters would. It took some time for Sonya to trust Kelsey enough to tell her of her horrible home life. When she did, Kelsey sat in stunned silence for minutes before bursting into tears and clutching Sonya to herself in sympathy. Sonya had never felt this kind of caring or expressions of affection before from anyone but her mom, and merely hugged Kelsey back while discovering and wondering in the comfort being extended to her.

Then, things took a turn to the horrific. Sonya had just turned seventeen, and routinely locked herself in her room when she got home from school. One evening when Erica was just finishing up in the kitchen Crummy came in, grabbed her by the arm, and dragged her back into the TV room where two of his buddies where smoking and getting high. The meth crystals were strewn on the table and everyone in the room had that glassy-eyed look of soon-to-be brain-dead indulgence. This time, however, the atmosphere was openly threatening. Crummy wanted to show his pals what a beauty she was. One of his pals grabbed her arms and Crummy tore off her blouse.

"Okay, guys, she's all yours. I hope this will be payment enough for the meth and the pipe."

"Should be, Crummy. Ya think she will stay awake long enough for the three of us?"

"She will, or I'll make sure she will."

Crummy's pals proceeded to perform a vicious and degrading sexual assault as best they could in light of their drug-induced altered state. Erica struggled and screamed but couldn't escape the degradation while her husband laughed. Sonya had heard the noise, screams and yells. She snuck out of her room and edged down the hall to the TV room and peeked around the corner. What she saw made her gasp and pull back. She bit her hand to keep from screaming herself and drew the metallic taste of blood in her own mouth. The sight of her nearly naked mother being assaulted by strangers made her sick. She barely made it to the bathroom where she vomited. She ran back to her room and huddled in the corner. After recovering, somewhat, from the shocking scene, she called Kelsey on her cell phone and babbled and blubbered what she had just seen. Kelsey was badly shocked and deeply disturbed. "Did you call the cops?"

"No! What are they going to do?"

"Well, rape and assault are against the law! Call them, or I will!"

Sonya called 911 and managed to get the information out in between stammers. The dispatcher told her that a unit would be there in a few minutes. Sonya waited in abject terror.

Meanwhile, Crummy's buddies had finished with Erica, picked up their dope and left Crummy to clean up. Crummy dragged Erica into the bathroom and turned on the shower. He basically threw her into the shower stall and closed the glass door. He went back out and started putting his dope and weed away in his "secret" cupboard. Just then there was a knocking on the door as the police arrived.

"Open up! Police!"

"Wadda you assholes want?"

"We received a call of a domestic disturbance. Open up."

"Sure." The rapidly sobering Crummy Keller opened the door and greeted the two uniformed officers.

"What's your name? May we look around? Smells like you had some kind of party going on. Where is everybody?"

"Name's Cromwell Keller. They just left. Sorry about the mess. I haven't had a chance to clean up the beer bottles."

"The call in said that there was a gang rape going on. Do you have a wife?"

"Yup. She's in the shower. She don't like my friends. Who called you?"

"Sorry. Can't say. Please retrieve your wife. We need to speak with her."

Reluctantly, Crummy went to the bathroom, turned off the water and pulled Erica up off the floor of the shower stall. He forced her into her robe. She still seemed to be in a state of shock but was able to walk on her own.

"Ma'am. What is your name?"

No response.

"What is your name, ma'am?"

"Erica. Erica Keller."

"Are you okay?"

Crummy grabbed the back of her robe and gave it a little tug.

"Uh. Yes. I'm okay. It was a long day at the office."

"Ma'am, we received a call that there was a rape going on at this address. Do you know anything about it?"

"Uh. No. I took a shower after dinner." She couldn't disguise the look of horror and fear in her eyes and face. The two officers just looked at one another and then at Crummy. His sallow complexion and blood-shot eyes spoke volumes about his state of body chemistry. But without any proof or corroboration from any witnesses, they couldn't pursue the matter further.

"Does anyone else live here?" the senior officer asked.

"Yeah. Our daughter," Crummy said.

"May we meet her, please?"

"Nah. She's doing her homework."

"Sir, we need to speak with her. It won't take long, and we have to be thorough when answering domestic disturbance calls."

"There's no domestic disturbance. Maybe it's time for you to leave."

"Sir, we WILL speak with your daughter here, or at the station. Your choice."

With that, Erica broke free and went to Sonya's room, knocked and told her to come talk to the policeman. The women walked slowly back to the front room.

"Your name, miss?"

"Sonya."

"Did you call 911 to report a domestic disturbance?"

Crummy stapled Sonya with a menacing glare. The two officers noticed it and shared a glance of their own. Sonya turned pale and only croaked something incoherent.

"Do you have a cell phone, Sonya?" She nodded. "May we see it please?" She nodded and pulled it out of her hip pocket, handing it to the policeman.

Crummy's glare became downright ugly and he turned very red and foreboding.

The policeman scrolled through Sonya's "recent" application and saw the 911 call. He showed his partner and handed Sonya back her phone.

"Why did you call 911, Sonya?" Her knees were trembling, and she looked ready to faint.

"I, uh, I thought I saw something going on. Maybe I was just dreaming."

"So, you're saying that there was no rape in progress, is that right?"

"Uh, yeah. I guess so."

"Were you aware that making false alarms to 911 is a crime, Sonya?"

"Uh, no." The stricken look on her face gave the officers pause and they looked at each other again knowingly, signaling a dead end.

"Okay. Look, you people better sort yourselves out. It's clear that something happened here and you're trying to walk it back. Your names and address will be put on the alert board. Good night."

The officers left and as soon as the door slammed shut, Crummy grabbed Sonya and shook her almost senseless. "What do you mean calling the cops on us? We coulda got busted for drugs and other stuff. Let me tell you how it's gonna be now. When my buddies come over, you're going to be their plaything. If you so much as whimper, I'll beat you purple. I'm putting a padlock on your room door tomorrow and will only let you out when it's time for you to 'entertain' my pals. You got that? Gimme that damned cell phone!" He threw it on the floor and stomped it, crushing the face and the case. He then threw it into the trash. "You're not calling anybody ever again, got that?"

Sonya, in total shock, nodded dumbly. Crummy then spun her around and pushed her toward her room. But he wasn't done. He grabbed Erica next and repeated his threats. The look of fear on her face merely made Crummy's drug-addled brain feel even more justified in his reign of terror against the two women in his house. He was about to slap her around, but he was running out of energy. Instead, he pushed her away and took a beer out of the refrigerator and flopped on the couch, slurping noisily.

Erica came back to Sonya's room and held her sobbing, trembling daughter. "We gotta do something, baby. I can't protect you from this animal. Do you have a friend where you can go and hide?"

Between sobs, she said, "Maybe Kelsey. But what about you? He might kill you."

"I know. I'm working on it. There are shelters for battered wives. I'm gonna go to one tomorrow after I leave for work. Try to get some rest. See Kelsey at school tomorrow and see what she can do. Also, pack a getaway bag tonight. The first chance you get, make a run for it."

Sonya saw Kelsey at school and told her about last night and the threats. Kelsey held her sobbing friend for minutes in the girls' bathroom until she regained some composure. "Come over to our house whenever you need to. I'll call my mom and dad today and give them a heads-up as to your situation."

When Sonya got home from school the next day, Crummy's pals were waiting. There were three of the scuzziest-looking men Sonya had seen in her life. She'd never seen these three before. Sonya was dressed in her school clothes that included a white blouse under a thin sweater and a knee-length, plaid skirt. Before she could escape to her room, her father grabbed her and said, "Here she is, boys. Have fun." The three men jumped for Sonya as one. Her books went flying and they started ripping her clothes off.

With that, Crummy got everyone another beer and sat back to watch the show. Sonya's screams and cries were ignored as the three druggies took turns violating her. She tried to fight back but was way too weak to make any worthwhile resistance. Her long, lithe limbs were being held by the two men not "participating". After what seemed like an eternity to Sonya, the men just got up and went back to their seats. Crummy grabbed Sonya by the hair and dragged her to her room where he locked her in. Great gales of laughter emanated from the TV room as the four men reviewed the scene to each other.

Chapter 2

TRAINING

ERICA CAME HOME FROM WORK that fateful day and saw a padlock that Crummy had installed and locked on Sonya's bedroom door. "What the hell do you think you're doing? We're not your prisoners! Open this door and let her go!"

"She stays because she tried to rat me out. You're next, so shut the fuck up or I'll break your face."

That was the Rubicon that Erica knew would come. This bastard was NOT going to imprison her daughter. She banged on Sonya's door and told her to get out. Erica grabbed her coat, purse and getaway bag and bolted out the door before Crummy could stop her. She drove directly to the battered wives' shelter and told them the story, showed them the bruises from the other night's assault and told them he was holding Sonya captive. The women's shelter assigned Erica to a bed and called the police to report the incidents she had claimed.

Meanwhile, having heard this latest upheaval through the bedroom door, and Erica's directive to leave, Sonya, having dressed again, grabbed her getaway bag, opened her bedroom window and dropped the few feet to the ground. She had no phone, so she just ran as fast as she could toward Kelsey's house. By running and walking, it took less than half an hour to get there. Every fiber in her body screamed for escape from this nightmare. Every step was agony. Every breath, painful. The street signs blurred through her tears and her throat was painfully dry from the heavy breathing and sobbing.

Kelsey, waiting at her front door, received Sonya with open arms and allowed her to openly and loudly weep for the minutes it took to relieve the immediate horror of her recent experience and the subsequent kidnapping.

The police, responding to the call from the battered wives' shelter, arrived at the Keller home and arrested Crummy. When they made him unlock the bedroom door, they saw the window open and Sonya gone. They photographed the padlock and the open window. They also searched the premises and discovered Crummy's stash of drugs and paraphernalia. They packaged it up and took it with them and their handcuffed suspect to the city jail for booking.

Sonya had the look of a frightened, whipped dog. She was still trembling and had the wide-eyed stare of pure terror. With Kelsey's parents sitting nearby, she carefully coached Sonya to recount the recent events. As she talked, the details of her assault and rape became more vivid, dramatic and lurid. Everyone sat rapt and horrified. She ended up curled in a ball on the couch trembling and mumbling. The Morrows recognized that there was significant psychological damage as well as the physical injuries. It reminded Ned Morrow, Kelsey's father, of his training in PTSD recognition while in the Navy. Sonya's story and terrified presentation impacted the entire Morrow family at once and their hearts reached out to her. "What are you going to do?" Ned asked. "Where is your mother?"

After a long pause, Sonya quietly whispered, "I don't know. I have no place to go and I can't go to school, because he'll find me. I think my mother ran to a battered wives' shelter. I don't know which one. Everything's been happening so fast."

"Okay. You'll stay here until things get sorted out," Ned said.

The Keller house became a crime scene, so neither Sonya nor Erica could get in to retrieve their clothes and personal items. They were out with virtually just the clothes on their backs and their getaway bags. Cromwell Keller was charged with drug possession the next day and held in the jail. Further charges would have to wait until Erica and Sonya could give a statement.

After a night's rest, Ned and Evelyn canceled their schedules and tried to gently talk Sonya down from her very bad place. "Who were the other men?" Ned asked.

"I THINK I REMEMBER SOMEBODY named Jimmy something. The other guy was called 'Rooster'. I think the third guy had a street name that sounded like 'Demon'."

"Do you remember what they looked like?" asked Evelyn.

"Oh yes! I'll never forget their faces." She started to sob, "I was so weak. I tried to fight back, but they were too strong. I couldn't get away. They really hurt me."

"Okay, Sonya. First, I want to get you to a hospital and have you checked out for internal injuries. We'll notify the police while we're there. They'll probably order a rape kit done at that time. Next, we'll wait for the police to come and take your statement. It will help get your father what he deserves. Finish your breakfast, then we'll get going. Don't shower or clean your body parts. The rape kit will be more complete with the collected DNA from your attackers. Do you understand?"

"Yes. Thank you for taking me in. I wouldn't have the first idea what to do. I'm scared out of my mind."

"Don't worry, Sonya," Evelyn said. "We've seen stuff like this before down South. We'll do our best to get you back on your feet and get you and your mother some justice too."

Ned Morrow was raised outside Birmingham, Alabama by a sharecropper and his wife. Ned was the youngest of four brothers and a sister. The parents insisted that their very bright son, Ned, would go to college. But after the first 2 years at the University of Alabama, the money just wasn't there, and Ned had to drop out. He joined the Navy, and because of his intelligence, physical strength and athleticism, a chief steered him toward SEAL (sea, air, land acronym) school in Coronado, California. There was nothing as demanding and strenuous as SEAL school, but Ned Morrow graduated second in his class. He became an expert at hand-to-hand fighting with fists and weapons of various sorts. His quickness and technique were the envy of his entire class. Added to these skills was Ned's inherent physical strength. Sure, everybody lifted weights, but Ned broke the lift weight and repetition records at SEAL school...by a lot. His instructors were amazed but pushed him even harder during training and simulated mission exercises. They conspired to see what Ned could actually do and were never disappointed by an average outcome.

Ned Morrow spent several more years as part of SEAL teams that performed very secret black operations that he could never discuss...ever! He also spent some time in sniper school and became an expert marksman with several weapons under severe conditions of camouflage and concealment. Ned Morrow became America's ultimate combat weapon. Everyone expected Ned to re-up and become an officer that trained other SEALS.

But Ned had other ideas. He wanted to finish college and the G.I. Bill would help him do that. He felt that more education would lead him to his life's work, something yet undecided. He had no idea how important that decision would be. He returned to the U. of Alabama and finished his degree in criminal justice and counseling. He kept physically fit and even worked part-time at a karate *do-jo* to keep his skills sharp. He also discovered that he was a good teacher. Nobody could challenge him in skills and strength, but he refused to enter competitions. His vision for martial arts saw people needing the skills and motive to keep themselves fit and to defend themselves against assault from criminals and other very bad people. He came to specialize in teaching women the skills and agility necessary to thwart attackers under any situation. As his reputation spread, the demand for his services increased throughout Huntsville, Alabama. The *do-jo there* hired him part-time to teach women's defense classes and paid him enough where he could live on his own.

During one of his self-defense classes, he met a new student named Evelyn Childers. She was exceptionally bright and wanted to learn *everything* all at once. Evelyn was not petite, but a well-proportioned 5 feet, 9 inches. Ned was just barely 6 feet, so it wasn't unusual for them to partner up for techniques practice. Ned observed that Evelyn lacked the physical strength and muscle development to do the things the discipline required. He wrote up a training regimen for her and told her to either buy some weights or use a gym somewhere. Since she was also in college, she used the school gyms to work on her strength. She had to go to off-hours workouts as black women were not allowed into the weight room while white students were present. After a few months, Evelyn Childers became the star student in Ned's *do-jo.*

To Ned, Evelyn's beauty grew more alluring every day. Her keen intelligence, brilliant, seductive smile and flashing dark eyes attracted him as a bee to a flower. Before too much more time passed, they were having coffee or sodas after class. He ran into her on campus one day and he bought her lunch. Thus began a romance of mutual attraction of personalities and, eventually, a passionate, loving, physical relationship. A month after Ned graduated from Alabama, he and Evelyn married to the everlasting joy of both their sets of parents. Their parents were terrified that Ned and Evelyn were each so far out of their depths in the local African-American community that they would never find a mate – and produce grandchildren.

Both families had had very unhappy experiences with prejudice, bigotry and, on two occasions, the KKK. Their trust in white people, in general, was very low. They had to endure the worst of times during the Jim Crow periods in the South, and were even too afraid to vote lest somebody put a flaming cross in their yard to scare the daylights out of them, burn their house down, or worse.

Evelyn finally graduated from the University of Alabama with a teaching degree and a sociology emphasis. She cast her bread upon the water looking for a teaching job... somewhere. Her credentials, grades and letters of reference were all very good, so her applications across the country were answered by many schools, but most asked her to come, at her own expense, to their campuses for interviews. The phone rang one day, and Evelyn found herself speaking to the dean of the education department at Northwestern University in Evanston, Illinois. After the lengthy interview, the dean offered her a part-time teaching position in her department. The pay wasn't great, but it was more than she was making working board jobs at school and waiting tables in the local bars. Ned thought he could find work as an instructor just about anywhere there were karate studios. After surveying the general area around the Chicago/Indiana border, *anywhere* turned out to be Gastonburg, Indiana. A small studio that was owned and operated by an elderly Japanese immigrant named Haiko Suzuki. *Sensei* Suzuki was only 5 feet, 6 inches tall, but was still solidly built with a head of thinning, gray hair. His face had plenty of character and age lines, but his sharp, dark eyes were almost sparkling with awareness. He also wore a thin mustache that drooped just to his chin line from his upper lip.

After a thorough and congenial, in-person interview, Ned submitted his credentials, awards and certificates by mail. *Sensei* Suzuki called Ned a few days later and offered him the position of assistant.

It would be a manageable commute to Northwestern for Evelyn, even though she had to traverse the city of Chicago both ways. BUT, it was cheaper to live in Indiana.

Ned started conducting classes at the *Midwest Martial Arts Studio* in

Gastonburg. As time passed, Mr. Suzuki gave more and more classes and tasks to Ned.

As they became better acquainted, Ned learned that *Sensei* Suzuki was the son of Okinawan parents. During the World War II battle for that island, those parents left Haiko standing on the cliffs above the crashing sea. As the American troops approached them, they reached for Haiko, but a soldier grabbed him just as his parents leaped to their deaths on the rocks below. He was taken into protective custody by the Americans and put in a holding camp on Okinawa until the war ended. A young American nurse took a liking to young Haiko and started the paperwork process to adopt him. When that process finished, the nurse, Mary Stanton, was sent to the main Japanese island, Honshu. There, she worked in a military hospital while trying to raise her son. The Navy provided childcare, and young Haiko, who the doctors surmised was about four years old, was put into a child learning program there too. After 2 more years of service, the Navy shipped Mary back home to Indiana where she continued to raise Haiko as an American boy.

MARY STANTON NEVER DID MARRY, and as she grew in her profession as a civilian, she was able to afford nice things for herself and Haiko. As Haiko grew, he accepted Mary Stanton as his new parent as memories of his birth parents and Okinawa slowly faded. Haiko was a gentle soul, but also possessed a fire for learning and expressing himself. For his twelfth birthday, Mary took them both back to Japan to visit the now re-built country so devastated by American bombs during the war. They spent 2 weeks touring the countryside more than the cities. Haiko loved the rural ambience and asked if he could stay. Mary was both hurt and intrigued by his request, and tearfully made a compromise with him. She would send him to boarding school in Japan for 6 months and bring him back to Indiana for the other half of every year until he came of age to decide for himself where he wanted to live and what he wanted to do.

It was while he was in Japan that Haiko Suzuki learned Japanese and the martial arts. His *sensei* turned out to be a very sage and skilled teacher of not only karate, but the code of *Bushido*, the warrior way. The Zen Buddhist personal philosophy complemented everything else Haiko learned while in Japan. Even though he struggled with the transitions every year, the formal schooling in America allowed Haiko to straddle both cultures, but his heart beat more fervently in Japan. After he graduated from his American high school, he returned to Japan where he met and married a lovely woman named Kioki Yamata. Haiko now worked for his *sensei* and earned a decent living. Kioki taught school in her village where they lived, about 50 kilometers west of Tokyo. Their relationship could only be described as loving and warm. In private they were bonded by the principles of equality and fairness, while in public, they had to maintain the traditional appearance of male superiority.

Then, on one rainy night, Kioki was struck by a speeding car and killed. To say that Haiko was devastated would not come close to the pain and heartbreak that covered him like an ever-tightening ligature of grief. Mary flew him back to Indiana for consolation. In her warm, emotionally comforting presence, Haiko regained his spirit and began to once again read and practice his arts. After about 6 months of emotional healing, he found his way to a dilapidated karate studio in a strip mall there in Gastonburg, Indiana. He entered and looked around at the very unclean and unkempt facility and saw nothing but opportunity. The owner was an ex-Marine who actually fought on Okinawa, stayed, learned karate and came home to open his own business. Now, as he aged, he became imprisoned by alcohol and let his business slide into disrepair as he did the same with his life.

Haiko went home to ask Mary if she would loan him the money to buy this studio and fix it up to resemble the one he trained in in Japan. Since her savings had grown over the years, it was an easy decision and they both rolled up their sleeves and turned *The Midwest Martial Arts Studio* into a gleaming jewel of cross-cultural beauty and purpose. Mother and son grew the business with Mary, now a retired professional nurse, applying her significant energy and skills into the business side of things while her resilient son organized classes, built exercise/weight rooms, showers and even a small sauna. And so Haiko Suzuki came to be a very successful studio operator and gentleman of the highest caliber. Meeting and hiring Ned Morrow created a sense of culmination in Haiko's life; it was like turning over the business to a son, the son he never had. As the two men became close, Mr. Suzuki imparted upon Ned Morrow the elements of *Bushido* and Zen philosophy.

Eventually, Ned's reputation as a teacher and trainer found its way to members of the Chicago Bears football team. Three of the players hired Ned full-time to train them all year long. They were also interested in learning some martial arts, and Ned's business career blossomed from there. Mr. Suzuki retired after Ned had worked there for 2 years. He retained ownership but turned the entire business over to Ned. He advised Ned to save up his money for a down-payment when he decided to sell the business. Mr. Suzuki had no living family in the United States, so he had no place or person to whom he could will his studio. He told Ned that the sooner he could afford the down-payment, he would take his money and return to Japan. At the time of Sonya's escape, Ned had owned the studio outright for 10 years.

Kelsey was born 2 years after Ned and Evelyn were married and struggling to make ends meet. When the Chicago Bears players contracted with Ned, things became much simpler. Kelsey, it turned out, was exceptionally bright and curious; no surprise considering her parents' intellect and skill sets. Her parents' biggest challenges in her upbringing involved keeping her in enough books so she would not become bored. By the time Kelsey went to middle school, for example, she had finished reading Arthur Conan Doyles' complete works of Sherlock Holmes. Kelsey also picked up athletics quickly. Her dad played hand-eye coordination games with her from the beginning. She could dribble a basketball without looking at it by the time she was six. Her hands weren't that big, but she had a great feel for the ball. Ned also played catch with her using a regulation baseball. That ended when Kelsey missed a lob from her father, and it smacked her in the mouth.

By the time Sonya and Kelsey became friends, Kelsey was taking advanced algebra, chemistry and government classes, only offered to the most exceptional students in tenth grade. Sonya had virtually no home-taught study skills as her parents were quite dysfunctional during virtually her entire childhood. Kelsey tutored Sonya in a way that didn't intrude on their friendship and, in fact, enhanced it. Sonya had no idea about her own intelligence or scholastic abilities until Kelsey showed her how to study and how much fun learning new stuff every day could be. The attention and focusing skills ended up being the most precious gift Sonya received from her now best friend. Kelsey was an upbeat, friendly, pretty and fun-loving young lady. She infused everything she did with humor and fun. Sonya was the perfect foil for those things that allowed her to lighten her emotional load that she carried with her from her former existence.

Ned, Evelyn and Kelsey took Sonya to the police station where she was directed to the clinic for examination and the rape kit procedure. The police then reunited Erica with Sonya after learning of the battered women's home from the day before. After seeing the doctor, Sonya and Erica both gave their depositions to the detectives assigned to their case. Erica's and Sonya's depositions were interrupted often with tears and choked voices. Having to relive the events of the last few days sent the women back into a spiral of fear, hate and pain. Erica, the Morrows and Sonya agreed that Sonya should stay with the Morrows. Erica would put the house up for sale (years earlier, she had smartly gotten Crummy to agree to a quit-claim deed giving her power of attorney should Crummy not be available for real estate transactions), and find a place to live, then bring Sonya home to her new place. The women returned to the crime scene and took only what they needed to pack and extract temporarily until Erica could get set up in a new place. They collected their personal items and went to their respective sanctuaries. Erica wasted no time getting a real estate agent involved with the sale as soon as the police took the tape off the doors.

It took a few days before Sonya was able to stop being fearful and more fully accepting of the emotional support that Ned, Evelyn and Kelsey were bestowing on her as trusted friends and protectors. One day during the next week, Ned took Sonya shopping for some good running shoes and workout clothes. Her mood brightened immediately, and she asked Ned to take her for a run as soon as they finished shopping. Sonya took off like a frightened filly – which she was – and made Ned strain a little to keep up. But Sonya's lack of physical conditioning brought her back to jogging speed after less than half a mile, panting deeply. Ned began the quiet instruction and coaching that made him such a success with his clients. "Try not to gasp from your exertion. Try to measure your breaths both deep and shallow. You're gonna be fine, but it'll take some time for you to become conditioned where you can run longer distances." He coaxed her into a comfortable, relaxing gait. Soon she was in a groove, but only lasted another mile before her legs gave out.

"Ned, I have a long way to go, don't I? Didn't you tell me that when you were a SEAL, you guys ran 5 miles every morning?"

"Yep. And by the time we were in training for just a month or so, we hardly breathed hard at all. After the run the *really* hard part of the training started. Baby, we were so tired, some of us fell asleep at evening chow. I don't expect you to get into that kind of shape."

With her hands on her knees, she looked up at Ned and smiled for the first time since she'd arrived after that horrifying night. "Maybe not, but I've got to get stronger and be able to run more."

They walked back to the house talking about training and getting stronger. Sonya couldn't shake the feelings of helplessness she endured during her recent horror. The germ of making herself into someone who would never be so weak again began to grow into a compulsion. The tragic spark of her and her mother's abuse at the hands of desperately damaged men lit a fire in her that grew in strength and brightness daily, burning most hotly when recalling the laughing faces of the rapists...and her father.

Sonya ventured to Ned's basement weight room the next day and started trying to lift some weights. There were charts on the wall showing certain exercises and there was a kind of universal machine upon which she could work every muscle group in her body. Again, due to lack of conditioning, she petered out quickly after only a few repetitions. According to the charts, she learned to recover between "sets" of each exercise, but after one half hour, her muscles were exhausted, stiff and weak. "I've got to get in better shape!" she exclaimed aloud to herself.

That night, she asked Ned to make her a training program. She also agreed to do the schoolwork required by the homeschool programs of Indiana. Since Evelyn was a certified teacher in both Illinois and Indiana, she was tasked with developing the lessons necessary for Sonya to complete her high school diploma requirements and could sign off on Sonya's programs and examinations for the necessary credits toward graduating high school. Erica, still living in a battered women's shelter, agreed to this arrangement and signed the required forms. To earn her "keep" at the Morrow household, Sonya agreed to do the housework, the yard work, laundry and grocery shopping while she learned how to cook. Thus began the transformation of a terrified, abused girl into a well-balanced, physically enabled young woman.

The next day, of course, Sonya could barely get out of bed without hurting from her protesting muscles that let her know they'd been abused. When she asked Ned why she was so sore from the gym workout, he told her things she never imagined or thought about. Ned dusted off one of his old textbooks that showed pictures of what muscle tissue looked like. The microphotographs showed long, striped fibers lying parallel to one another and depicting the relaxation and contraction state of skeletal muscle. "You mean there are different kinds of muscles?"

"Yes. There are *three* kinds. One is heart muscle that is kind of self-stimulating; that's a good thing. If it weren't, we couldn't circulate our blood. The kind your feeling all over today is called *skeletal* muscle. See? It looks like strings lying side by side. The third kind is called *visceral* or *involuntary* muscle. Sometimes it's called 'smooth' muscle because it doesn't show the stripes you see in the heart and skeletal muscle cells. The stripes, by the way, are called *striations.* Smooth muscle is found in your arteries, digestive system and even your uterus. In fact, the uterine muscles are the strongest in your body; they have to contract to expel the baby when it's due. Anyway, the reason your muscles are so sore is because when you strain them past what they're used to, tiny bits of blood escape from the small blood vessels supplying the muscles with the chemicals they need to operate. These tiny blood drops clot into semi-solid micro-lumps and irritate the nerves nearby. See, without those *sensory* nerves to tell your brain how much or how little you need to contract or relax those muscles, you wouldn't be able to do *anything.* And they also register the discomfort you're feeling."

"Wow! I had no idea."

"Yeah, most people don't, but if you want me to train you, you're going to know everything. It'll make you a smarter athlete and give meaning to what you're doing here in the gym. Now, put on your running shoes so we can stretch out some of that soreness and get in a run before dark."

As autumn gave way to winter, Sonya's training became more indoors than outdoors in nature, but noticeable differences in her body's form impressed everyone. She was now able to lift and use greater weights than any woman Ned had ever trained, including Evelyn and Kelsey. She added running stadium stairs with weighted belts to expand her leg strength, speed and endurance.

Meanwhile, Erica saved up enough to get an apartment big enough for Sonya's return. The house sold after a few months on the market, giving Erica the small amount of equity it had earned, even though the local economy was not doing well. Local jobs had been sent to other countries and layoffs were everywhere.

"I like the apartment, Mom. My bedroom is bigger than the one at the house. Nice kitchen. Evelyn and Kelsey are teaching me how to cook, so I'll whip up some real gourmet meals for you when you get home from work."

"Oh, that'll be something to see," Erica said through a laugh. "I'll settle for things not burned or raw."

"Not to worry. So, when do we move in?"

Just after the new year arrived, Sonya asked Ned if she could start learning the martial arts. She'd been to the studio several times to watch Ned work out and teach his classes. "Of course you can. It will give you more agility, flexibility and quickness in everything you do," he told her. He began with the simple lessons of punching and kicking, but not before she learned to stretch, breathe and respect the art instead of the associated violence. She soon started working on the heavy punching bag with punches and kicks. With each passing week, it seemed the sound from her blows got louder and sharper. She was ready for the next phase of her training. For her eighteenth birthday, Ned, Evelyn and Kelsey took Sonya shopping for new outfits. Her growing musculature was straining the seams of her older clothes and it was time to get her properly fitted.

One day, Sonya went to Ned's studio where she watched his students practicing throws, punches and blocks of various types. She especially focused on the women's defense class later in the day. She asked to participate and jumped right in only to find herself flying through the air and landing with thuds as the more advanced students took their turns showing her how to defend against various assaults and attacks. One lesson got quite physical giving Sonya a bloody nose. The students all applauded as she recovered from her first "combat" injury.

The soreness from the bruises Sonya felt the next day was worse than after her first day of weight training. Blue spots appeared here and there. She HAD to learn this stuff. The pain made it even more obvious that being a victim was not on the menu any longer. She realized that all winners eventually get where they find ways to overcome adversity and prevail. Somehow the "art" of martial arts seemed quaint, especially after waking from yet another nightmare associated with her horrifying assault and rape from almost a year ago. She burned to see her attackers and her father pay some price besides just being fed by taxpayer-provided meals and shelter. Each time these thoughts and visions crossed her mind, she felt a seething rage that she struggled to keep just below the surface. These feelings and thoughts burned in her mind as she pumped her iron, ran her stairs and pounded the bags. There was another transformation occurring, but it was coming slowly and was hardly noticeable until something happened in the springtime that changed everything.

Sonya, Ned and Kelsey were out jogging briskly on an equally brisk April day when Sonya felt the need to test herself. "I'll race you to that corner by the traffic light," she blurted. The light was two blocks away and even though they'd already run 3 miles, Sonya felt energized.

Ned Morrow was a superb athlete, but when Sonya took off for the corner, he couldn't catch her. *Whoa!* he thought. *This is something special.* He took Sonya to his gym when they got home and took out the measuring tape. He measured her height, biceps, calves, thighs and waist. She measured at exactly 5 feet, 11 inches. Her limb circumference measurements were well-above average for American adult women, but not body-builder big. And she was dense! The scales showed her weighing in at one hundred-seventy pounds. Not believing his eyes and scale, he weighed himself to calibrate. It was accurate. He weighed Sonya again and the one-seventy number repeated. "Let's go out back and test your vertical," he said. Sonya's musculature showed very sharp definition but wasn't bulky or knotty looking. She had "6-pack" abdominal muscle definition and hips on the narrow side. Her legs were long and–well-muscled with the thigh and calf muscles in perfect proportion to each other. When she walked, everything rippled, but not in an unattractive or masculine way.

Even after the run and the sprint, Sonya hit 37 inches of air clearance. *This* absolutely astonished Ned. This eighteen-year-old girl was approaching Olympic athlete numbers. Thirty-seven inches was in the neighborhood of world-class female long jumpers. *No way Sonya was a high jumper*, he thought. *Too heavy*. The next day, Ned took Sonya and his stopwatch to the high school running track before the track team came out to train. He and Sonya stretched and jogged a couple laps. When she was fully recovered, he said he would time her in 100 meters. "Just stride out and do what you did yesterday in our little race," he said smiling.

He started the watch after yelling "GO" and stopped it as she passed him at the finish line. She hadn't started from a sprinter's crouch in blocks, but Ned's watch said 11.4 seconds. WHAT!

"Let's do it again. I don't think I timed it right. This time, start from a sprinter's stance."

"What's that?"

"Oh. Sorry. Let me show you. Okay. Let me get down to the finish line, and when I drop my arm, you start. I forgot about the time delay for my voice to reach you."

On this trial, Ned's watch said 11.0 seconds. "Oh. Oh. Sonya. What ARE you doing?"

Ned ran a few more trials at 100 and 200 meters with more astonishing results. He started thinking he had a world-class athlete on his hands. And she was BIG. Almost 6 feet tall at one-hundred seventy pounds. There were wide receivers in the NFL with that size and speed. *DAMN*!

Ned let Sonya rest a while and, knowing she recovered from her workouts very quickly, asked her to run four laps of the track, or about a mile. "How fast should I run?" she asked.

"As fast as you think you can for the whole mile. You won't be sprinting, of course, but you should find a pace where you feel strong through the first three and a half laps. For the final 200 meters, you should let it all out and kick to the finish. Let's see what you can do."

Sonya blistered the first lap in 54 seconds, then eased back. Her long-legged stride gobbled up the distance. At 800 meters she timed out at 2 minutes, 4 seconds. Finally, with 200 meters to go, Sonya kicked into another "gear" and sprinted to the finish. For the first time, Ned saw her straining as she neared the line. Click! Four minutes, 15 seconds. In a way, Ned felt a little frightened by what he was seeing. This was only 3 seconds off the world record for women. Was this girl a super athlete or a superhero?

Ned and Sonya became great training pals. Kelsey was fit, strong and agile, but she couldn't keep up. Sonya and Kelsey also played one-on-one basketball games when they could. When Sonya dunked over Kelsey one day, the girls just looked at each other and started laughing until tears rolled down their faces. As the weeks passed, Sonya's strength and endurance kept improving. She was able to do thirty chin-ups with both hands and fifteen each with one hand. The entire Morrow family would gather in amazement to watch her work the weights.

She was also learning the moves, throws and personal defense techniques through the hybrid judo/karate techniques that Ned developed himself and taught at his *do-jo* such that she was ready to start testing for belts. Ned was especially impressed with Sonya's work ethic. At times, she seemed driven by some force he couldn't see, but her grunting and grinding on each exercise showed him that she had a much higher drive and purpose than just self-defense. She *attacked* each maneuver with a kind of viciousness Ned saw only during his time as a SEAL. "You should back off a little, so you don't injure yourself, Sonya. Too much max effort can weaken your joints at the same time it strengthens your muscles. You've got plenty of power without trying to pound the stuffing out of the big bags, or your classmates."

"I KNOW, BUT ONCE I get started, my mind and body shift into overdrive. I want to earn the belts as an accomplishment. You know, I've never really accomplished much. I have nothing to show for anything I've done so far. I'm trying to be a good student. Help me be the best at this I can be."

"Oh, I'll help you where I can, baby, but you're moving past the skill levels so fast, I have trouble keeping the lessons pertinent. You'll get those belts. I just want you to stay in one piece."

They both laughed at that tension-breaking joke. Sonya stripped off her gloves and toweled off. The hot shower felt soothing and drained the fatigue from her whole body. *Another day closer to getting those belts,* she thought to herself. *I've got to keep pushing. The demons inside won't let me rest.*

As Ned continued to work with his star pupil, he transferred some of his learnings of *Bushido* and Zen to Sonya. He wanted her to not only respect the art, but also to understand its origins and the state of mind that accompanied the physical aspects.

She went through the belt color tests very quickly. Her size, strength, intelligence and focus pushed her to the head of every class Ned taught. She was finally ready for her first-degree black belt and astonished everyone in the house, including the judges with her speed, agility and technique. Ned began to wonder if there was anything this girl couldn't do. On her nineteenth birthday, Ned and Evelyn bought Sonya a new *gi* (martial arts outfit) and a trip for her and Erica to join them in Las Vegas to watch the world karate championships that year. Ned thought that Sonya would probably do very well in her own right. Maybe next year.

Everyone returned to Gastonburg with a sense of relief and anticipation for Sonya's martial arts capabilities. During the national competition, Sonya was focused and enthralled with what she saw. The flashing of her eye contact with Ned told him how much she meant to drive herself to the levels of the champions she just watched. Ned had the sense that if she was a racehorse, he should be tightening his grip on the reins.

Chapter 3

THE DEFENDER

THE WHEELS OF JUSTICE PUT Crummy Keller in state prison for 2 years on drug charges. The rape kit had yielded enough DNA evidence to convict James "Jimmy" Raymond, Kevin "Rooster" Lock and Albert "Demon" Smith and send them to the same prison also for 2 years each for the rapes. The jury took exactly one hour to reach a unanimous conviction. There was insufficient direct evidence to convict these three of drug charges, so Crummy took the fall alone for being in possession of them. Erica and Sonya had to re-live the incidents when they testified in court and in their own minds when they read the news in the local paper, the *Gastonburg Gazette*.

The lurid story actually kicked off a series of investigative stories about the growing drug culture in not only Gastonburg, but throughout Indiana. The investigations listed hundreds of children being destroyed by the allure of mind-altering and organ-destroying street drugs like crack cocaine and methamphetamine. Opioids were addicting people of all ages. The perpetrators of this "industry" turned out to be very bad people with no sense of community, compassion nor respect for the rule of law. The legitimate drug companies were also emphasizing marketing and sales of so-called *legal* drugs like the opiates. Their only common interest was money and they organized themselves to make as much of it as they could as quickly as they could at the expense of everyone they could find to buy and dispense their products. The street dealers were mostly poor kids from troubled neighborhoods who wanted to earn and flash some easy money. Equally sad was that many of their customers buying the cheapest drugs were also from poverty-stricken places and looked to the drugs as an escape from their personal pain and hopelessness. The average education level of both the street-level criminals and the poor customers was below tenth grade. Needless to say, the articles suggested, the chronic underfunding of public schools by so-called conservative politicians contributed to the breakdown of purposeful education in these pockets of poverty.

On a parallel track, however, was the up-scale drug trade where middle-class and upper-class buyers led the way for even more money making for the street dealers and their organizations up the ladder. It was not unusual to see sleek, late model expensive cars cruising the drug neighborhoods to score a buy of some drug, from heroin, to opioids, to powder cocaine to the high-end crystal "meth" that ensured a rush of perceived joy among the idle millennials who thought doing drugs was a cool pastime. Even though they knew that the chemicals they were putting into their bodies destroyed brain cells and organ tissue, they didn't seem to care. They were young, rich, good-looking and unattached to the realities of the drug trade or the poverty that drove the sellers and their organizations. These young people deluded themselves into thinking they could live forever, and let the devil take the hindmost. Since their parents were so busy working at high-paying, but demanding jobs, the children received little parenting once they could function on their own. It was easier and more convenient for those parents working 60 hour per week jobs to give their kids a few hundred dollars to entertain themselves however they wished. They did this under the illusion that they'd done such a great job as parents by providing wealth and comfort, that nothing could possibly go wrong. While the parents remained willfully ignorant of the drug problem, the kids just didn't care that they were contributing, in sum, to the destruction of large parts of the American way of life, its culture and society in general. They represented the ultimate model of self-indulgence and self-absorbed, self-centered white (mostly) privilege.

The series of articles received many accolades from around the state including from the politicians in Indianapolis. Everybody was against the drug trade...or were they? As with just about any other cash-heavy industry, the drug trade also had its lobbyists who cajoled, bribed and purchased influence among those very politicians. Judges were compromised and the felony convictions were directed more toward the poor street dealers than the silk-suited upper echelons of the trade. Some politicians were paid just enough to look the other way. The last article in the series touched on this aspect of the drug scourge making several prominent politicians very nervous. There was a great beating of chests and spontaneous press conferences from these politicians leaving the interested observer to recall something from *Hamlet: Me thinks the lady doth protest too much.*

Sonya read the newspaper series with great interest. Anger again welled up inside her as she realized that everyone associated with the drug culture and its industry was actively destroying the country. . . and had robbed her of a father, her self-respect and left a terrified mother and daughter in its wake. As she read each part, the horror of her rape and humiliation reared up in her mind and mind's eye as recurring nightmares even in her waking hours. Mental pictures of her mother's bruised body and face were haunting, but the images of those three rapists grinning lasciviously at her as they enjoyed themselves at her expense haunted her constantly. Her father's cackling laughter at her screams and struggles echoed in her mind like some horrid scene from a bad movie.

She and her mother obviously had first-hand knowledge and experience with how drugs destroy a family unit. When Sonya visited the Morrows for workouts and her school lessons, she learned that they too were very concerned, upset and fearful that the drugs would find their way into Kelsey's life. Some of her friends at school had been hauled out on stretchers for overdosing in the bathrooms. And this was in an upper-middle class neighborhood school! Kelsey recounted how she saw kids in the lunch lines opening their purses and wallets revealing hundred-dollar bills. Kids were carrying around hundreds of dollars in cash! Why? During an open-house at the school, one of Kelsey's teachers told a room full of shocked parents, that included Ned and Evelyn, that her students told her they could get any drug she wanted and be back in class before lunch. The parents had NO idea that drug dealers were within walking/calling distance of their children in schools they thought were safe.

Then, one day just before the school year ended, Kelsey, jogging home from school, was attacked by three boys and had her money stolen. She was badly beaten and incurred a broken collarbone, a mild concussion and several minor cuts and bruises. She put up a fight but was eventually overpowered by the three boys. When they finished beating her, they stole her wallet, but left her phone. She crawled over to her backpack, pulled out the phone and called 911. She then called her father at the studio. He arrived just as the ambulance pulled up to the curb. Kelsey was sitting up on the curb trying to relieve the pain from her broken collarbone. Ned rushed to her side and tried to comfort her. A police unit showed up at this time and the two uniformed officers took her statement. She said she recognized the three boys and told the police who they were. They were among the poorer group of white kids at school and told the police that they wanted the money to buy drugs. After she gave them her statement, the EMTs loaded her into the ambulance and whisked her to the hospital.

Ned and Evelyn were devastated. Sonya was working out at the Morrows' home gym when Ned came home and told her what had happened. She was shocked, angry and again felt the burning fires of retribution eating at her soul. Tears burned in her eyes as she toweled off and quickly showered and changed into regular clothes. Was anyone safe from this scourge? Here, her dearest friend was beaten to within an inch of her life, so three bad kids could buy a few minutes of escape from their apparently painful lives. Whose life was more important was an easy question for Sonya to answer, and she started formulating an idea to correct the situation. Ned and Evelyn – who had just arrived after speeding home from school – took Sonya with them to the hospital to see Kelsey. She had just come out of X-ray and was receiving a tight shoulder harness to hold the bones in place while healing. The attending physician wanted to keep Kelsey under observation for a couple days while running tests to be sure she didn't have any serious internal injuries.

When they left Kelsey that evening, Sonya asked Ned about her becoming a Navy SEAL.

"Whoa. Why would you want to do that?" he asked.

"I want to learn how to work silently and lethally... uh, to defend my country against its enemies."

"Okay. Well, it will be very difficult for any woman to succeed and graduate as a SEAL, but if any woman can, you certainly will be able to handle the physical part of that school. You're smart enough to pass all the other tests too, but I worry about the psychological parts due to your trauma a couple years ago."

"Yeah. Maybe. Can you teach me to shoot? If the SEALS are too selective, maybe I'll just join the Army."

"I can teach you to shoot, if that's what you want? Have you given any thought about going to college?"

"I have, but my mom doesn't make enough even for a state school. We're just hanging on, and I really don't feel like going into debt from student loans. I'd still have to work part-time. If I join the military, I'll get education benefits while I'm in as well as when I leave. If I go in now, at eighteen, I'll be only thirty-nine when I get 20 years' service. That gives me full education and medical benefits for life. That's hard to pass up when things are the way they are.

"Thanks to you two, I'm going to graduate high school in January. I've passed all but the last few tests to get my diploma. I can't tell you how grateful I am to you and will make you proud of me, I promise."

Then, a kind of other-worldly gleam appeared in those large, robin's egg blue eyes. The look wiped the smiles off Ned's and Evelyn's faces as they felt an energy pulse from Sonya that they hadn't seen or felt before. As her jaw muscles pulsed, her eyes narrowed, and her lips became a thin, straight line. What was going on in her head?

Kelsey's recent attack by the druggie kids, and the scourge of illicit and harmful drug use – the gangsters and thugs inclusive – kept fueling her maturing desire to do something about it. She came to feel that the law was helpless in defeating the $5 billion industry of illegal drugs, so why should the law worry about a private citizen or two helping to eliminate some of the problem? She'd been pondering that thought train for some months now and moved the germination of a plan into full growth mode. Then, something happened that made that plan a lot clearer and more urgent.

One late afternoon in January, just before her high school final exams, Sonya ran home in the cold from Kelsey's house where she had been studying and working out. She had also practiced her throws and fighting skills with Ned at the studio earlier. When she walked into the apartment, she saw furniture in disarray, lamps on the floor and her mother... Erica was curled up on the floor near the coffee table clutching her ribs and moaning. When she looked up at the sound of Sonya entering the room, Sonya saw the bloody and bruised face of her mother looking bleakly at her. "What happened?" she yelled.

"It was Crummy. He got let out on probation and beat me up because I sold the house and put the money in the bank."

The divorce between Erica and Crummy had finalized about 2 months before Crummy got out on probation. Because of the power of attorney, Erica got sole possession of the title to the house and Crummy got ZERO visitation rights with Sonya.

"Did you call it in, yet?"

"It only happened an hour ago, I guess. I hurt so much..."

Sonya took out her phone and called the police. They arrived about 15 minutes later and started interrogating Erica. They called in a forensics team to collect evidence from Erica and the disheveled apartment. They said that the ambulance was on its way.

"He was wearing leather gloves and a leather jacket. He just started beating on me when I told him the house was sold. I don't know how he found out where I lived."

Sonya was seething. Her jaws were tightly clenched showing muscles working under the skin. "I'll bet he made somebody at the women's shelter tell him where you moved to. He probably offered somebody drugs to tell him, that bastard." Sonya was now trembling with rage, fire shooting from her narrowed eyes.

The police officers noticed and said, "We'll check into that. Good idea."

After the police left, Sonya said, "I'm going to find that son of a bitch and return some favors. But first we have to get you to the hospital and get you checked out."

"Oh, don't do that, baby. He'll hurt you, maybe even kill you." With that motherly warning, Erica hauled herself to her feet and let Sonya help her to the ambulance that had just arrived. Sonya rode with her.

"I'm not afraid of him, Mom. I've grown a lot and learned even more in the time he's been in jail. I can take care of myself."

"I know, but I just don't want you mixed up with that bastard."

"Sure. What car did he drive?"

"Something gray. I saw him drive up into the parking lot. It looked like an older car, maybe an old Chevy."

"Let me ask around. I'm sure the cops are doing that too."

After the ER doctor finished sewing up the cuts, the orderly rolled her up to ICU where she was monitored closely all night for any internal injuries. She was given a mild sedative to help her sleep and rest. She didn't need bad dreams waking her up.

The police gave Sonya a ride back home to the apartment where she went around to the neighboring apartments and asked about Crummy's car. All she got was that it was, in fact, an old gray Chevy and had a broken taillight. Next, she called Ned and asked if he knew somebody in the probation office in town.

"Could you find out where Cromwell Keller lives, Ned?"

"Maybe from one of my clients. What happened?"

When she told him what she discovered after getting home, it elicited a groan. "Oh, don't get involved with that guy. He probably has friends who will help him make big trouble for you and your mother. Leave it to the police."

"I know you're right, Ned, but you should see what he did to my MOTHER! Remember what he and his friends did to ME?" She was shouting now.

After a protracted silence, Ned said softly, "I understand. I'll see what I can do. Now go take care of your mother."

After hanging up, she straightened the apartment and cleaned up broken glass. She then drove over to the Morrows' to decompress. Ned and Evelyn hugged her and tried to encourage her. They told her that Kelsey's three attackers had been apprehended and arraigned in juvenile court. The judge sent them to juvenile detention for 6 months, then home with their parents. Somehow, that didn't seem right in view of the brutality of the attack. Ned and Evelyn relived some of the racially inspired injustices they experienced, and since the attackers were white kids, it affected them again with jaw-clenching frustration. Sonya picked up on that and suddenly felt guilty at being white. "Not all white people are like those little shits. Sometimes I'm ashamed of my whiteness when people like that are so evil."

"No, no, angel. You're not like any of those wicked and ignorant people who see nothing wrong with the double standard. You, of all people, do not need to shoulder any white guilt. This is something we've had to deal with for generations. It never seems to go away, but for black people to openly fight in a white-dominated world is asking for frustration or worse. Just be cool. We'll work the system. We KNOW how to do that."

One of Ned's clients was a criminal lawyer and Evelyn's legal representative at Northwestern. She knew who was working Kelsey's case through a friend at the local DA's office. They assured the Morrows that there was enough forensic and witness evidence to put these kids in some sort of confinement for quite a while. This wasn't their first offense.

After a cup of hot tea and some soothing conversation, Ned's phone rang. It was his probation officer friend. Ned wrote down something on a slip of paper and handed it to Sonya. "Be VERY careful, girl. Always remember your lessons about keeping the initiative and surprising your foe. And whatever you do, DO NOT attack the lethal areas. I know you want to exact your revenge, but you must do so without getting yourself in real trouble. My advice is to cut your hair short. Wear dark gray spandex and be sure your hands are protected and covered. Wear lightweight boots with hard toes. We love you very much and are frightened to death for you... but we understand what a low-life your father is and we worry that he will end up killing you AND your mother if he's allowed to. I've taught you well. You know what to do to render your target harmless for years to come."

The look of determination and focus Ned had seen on Sonya's face during matches against opponents was there now. Sonya had learned to bring that focus to a pinpoint and that, in addition to her physical capabilities, made her virtually unbeatable. Whoever ended up in her sights was in for big trouble. Ned hoped that he hadn't made a huge mistake, but trusted Sonya to implicate nobody else in whatever adventure she was about to pursue.

The address on the paper slip was located in a seedy part of town, perhaps 4 miles from her apartment. She drove the 2 miles home from the Morrows' and ate dinner, showered and laid out her outfit for the next day. It would be cold tomorrow, so she included the lightweight, insulated underwear she would wear under her top layers.

First thing next day, after a good night's sleep, Sonya drove to a local department store at a small mini-mall and looked for the spandex top and bottom. She found one in charcoal gray that hugged her body comfortably and allowed complete flexibility. The clerk called them "yoga outfits", but Sonya just smiled. Her next stop was the army surplus store where she bought face make-up and a flexible head covering, a balaclava. With packages in arms, she walked down to the hairdresser at the other end of the little mini-mall and had her beautiful, light brown, long tresses cut. The shop gave her a discount if she allowed the hair to be used in making wigs. No problem. Her new hairstyle was short enough to be off her collar but shaped to accentuate the features of her pretty face, complete with the deep dimples when she smiled.

She then drove over to the neighborhood of the address, careful to avoid passing the actual residence she had memorized. Sure enough, there was the gray Chevy with the broken taillight parked in the street. She parked on the nearest cross-street where she could see the door to the dingy apartment building where her target lived. Yes, in her mind she now categorized her own father as a target. His violence toward her mother and herself put him outside the sphere of family relationships and made him the evil enemy who seemed to do nothing but hurt people. That would soon change.

Just as these thoughts started to simmer, a police cruiser pulled up in front of the target's apartment. The two officers, hands resting on their weapons, banged on the door. After a short time, Crummy answered it dressed in faded jeans and a nondescript shirt. The cops went in and the door closed. A few minutes later, the police led Crummy out the door in handcuffs, but now he was wearing a leather jacket. Shit! The cops got to him first!

Frustrated, Sonya drove home and loaded all her new things into her closet and dresser. She glanced at the mirror as she passed the closet door and turned to look at her new hairdo. "Not bad," she said out loud. Since the rape, she had never paid much attention to her own looks or sexuality. The psychological damage had drilled down into her self-esteem psyche such that she had repressed her sex drive and attitudes toward men as lovers to the point of it never being part of her consciousness. The complete commitment to her physical training and development were her outlets. She only had room to love her mother and the Morrows. Other than that, she saw herself as Sonya, the defender... sort of. Now, however, with this last attack on her mother, she realized that the word *defender* had real meaning as well as being a bridge to action.

Chapter 4

THE FIRST MISSION

AFTER 2 WEEKS IN JAIL, Cromwell Keller's case came before the judge. Erica Keller did indeed press charges for the beating she received, but there was no physical evidence at the apartment that defined Crummy was the perpetrator, and the lawyer somebody else paid for managed to get witness testimony thrown out as hearsay and discredited the inconsistencies from those witnesses the police interviewed. Crummy was released on time served and returned to the jurisdiction of the parole office. When Erica told Sonya this news, she was furious. "He got off again with just a slap on the wrists?" she said in full voice. But, in her mind, Sonya once again saw her father as game in the field. It was time to execute the plan that she'd been working on for some time. It began with a greeting card.

The card had a picture of a cartoon character on the front. The inside was blank, so Sonya pasted cut-out letters and glued them, being sure to use rubber gloves while handling the card and its envelope. She used an old ink pen at the bottom of her desk drawer to address the envelope and used a press-on stamp. The pen then went into the kitchen trash bag for disposal the next day. The message read: *Hello, Crummy. Let's meet and talk about business. I'll be behind the kiosk at the park after ten on the tenth of February. See you there.* She drove to Gary and mailed it ensuring an out-of-town postmark.

The tenth of February was still a week away, so Sonya trained hard on the big bag and lifted weights with added effort. Kelsey was now home still recovering from her broken shoulder. She watched Sonya work out, but few words were exchanged. Sonya had that *look* of great intensity. She executed her kicks and spins with great effort and skill, while Kelsey held the big bag with her uninjured hand and arm. Kelsey could feel the breeze from Sonya's feet as they whizzed just millimeters from her head and face and the shock on the bag from her kicks and punches. Somebody was in for a big hurt.

"Wow! You're sure into it these days. Do you have a competition coming up?"

"Sort of. I just want to be as sharp as I can. I want to be at the top of my training."

"Oh, I wouldn't worry too much about that," Kelsey said with a chuckle. "You're already a beast."

"Maybe, but I don't want to give anything away too soon," she laughed. "I have a couple things to do first. By the way, thanks to you and your parents for the *daisho Samurai* sword set." The *katana,* or "long sword", had a gleaming, polished and razor-sharp blade with hand carved designs. The haft was beautifully wrapped in dark red cord with dragons drawn on the hand guard. The *wakizashi,* or "side arm" was the shorter weapon, but had patterns to match the *katana.* "Now, I'm going to have to start *kendo* classes somewhere so I can properly handle those beauties."

"Oh yeah? What are you going to use them on?"

"I dunno. I'm sure something will come up."

At about eight o'clock on the evening of the tenth, Sonya slowly got herself dressed. It was another very chilly winter night, so she wore the flexible thermal underwear right next to her skin and pulled on the yoga pants and top. She put on her new lightweight, black hiking boots that had hard rubber toes and soles. She packed the make-up, running shoes, a towel and balaclava in her backpack and grabbed a jacket. "I'm going over to

Kelsey's for a little while," she called to her mother, now home and healing. "See you later. Keep the doors locked."

"Bye, honey. See you later."

When she was on the street, she called Kelsey and informed her that she was coming over. She walked slowly and it took until about nine o'clock.

"It's a little late for a workout, Sonya," Kelsey said, opening the door.

"I won't be long. I just told my mom I was coming over. I've got some other errands to run, so can I make myself a cup of hot tea and let me use the toilet?"

"Sure. You know where everything is. Love the outfit. Where are you going with that rig?"

"Oh, I just want to have a good, long run on this cold night. Believe it or not, these two layers keep me pretty warm as long as I'm moving around."

Sonya gulped down the tea before it got too cool, hugged Kelsey and left after having spoken just a few words. The kiosk in the park had a restroom where Sonya went in and applied her make-up. She pulled the balaclava over her head and adjusted it making sure no white skin showed. Gastonburg had yet to install CCTV around the park, but Sonya wanted to be as invisible as she could anyway. She put on the black leather working gloves and cinched them tight. She stuffed her jacket into her backpack and hid it in the bottom of the waste bin, putting the plastic liner back over it. Where she would be standing, she could view the restroom door as well as see anyone who ventured into the cone of light thrown by the single, low-watt bulb at the rear of the kiosk.

At nine forty-five, she slowly opened the restroom door and slithered along the wall and into the shadows. She looped around so that she stood against a large tree trunk and faced the cone of light. She figured to be about 25 feet from the light and knew she would be invisible to anyone looking her way. The color of shadows is NOT black, but a dark gray, a perfect match for her tight-fitting outfit. She was ready.

The clock in a nearby steeple rang ten. Crummy was late. Did he send someone ahead to scout the area, or was he waiting to see who showed up? Sonya waited silently and immobile, dynamically contracting her muscles to keep warm while not moving any of her limbs. Finally, at about ten-fifteen, she heard a car door slam and saw the lank figure of Crummy Keller slowly walking over to the kiosk. His head was on a swivel. Of course, he would be suspicious. He stepped nearly into the light and kept looking in every direction. He hadn't seen her.

SONYA TOOK THREE STEPS TOWARD the light. He glimpsed some movement in the shadows and turned toward it reaching into his belt.

Before he could pull out his pistol, Sonya took two large running steps and leaped, spun in the air and delivered a perfectly aimed heel kick precisely to the point of Crummy's jaw. She recovered in mid-air and landed on her feet as Crummy crashed into the wall of the kiosk and sprawled on the cement. Sonya quickly leaped again and landed with both feet on his solar plexus which knocked every molecule of air from his lungs. He grabbed his abdomen and started to double up trying to breathe, but Sonya delivered another kick to his face with the hard toe of her boot. Blood flew and splattered the sidewalk. His breathlessness prevented him from screaming or calling out.

Now, it was time for the real damage to Crummy's anatomy. Sonya grabbed his right wrist and jerked it free. She then snapped his whole arm like a whip dislocating the shoulder. What followed was a knee drop in the back side of his elbow splintering the hinge joint so that it now bent both ways. A strange kind of strangled grunt emanated from Crummy's throat, but Sonya wasn't quite done. She looked around to make sure nobody was around and grabbed his right ankle. Her swift pivot brought his lower leg up to where she could perform another knee drop on *his* knee joint tearing all the ligaments in the process. She then stomped as hard as she could, bringing her one-hundred seventy pounds down on his left ankle. She repeated this action quickly until she heard bones break.

Crummy was now getting his wind back, so Sonya delivered another kick to his solar plexus and left him struggling once again against the excruciating pain she knew was blowing his brain apart. Silently she dashed to the restroom, retrieved her backpack and ran out of the park being sure to avoid being silhouetted against any background light. When she got to a quiet street, she began walking normally while she removed the balaclava and used the moist towel she brought along to wipe off the camouflage make-up. She put on her jacket and stuffed the balaclava and towel back in her backpack. When she passed a local restaurant behind which was a dumpster, she noticed that the employees were dumping trash at the end of the workday. She waited until they went in for another load, then tossed the make-up, the towel and her kicking boots into the depths of the waste bin. She ducked back into some shadows and put on the running shoes she'd brought just for this occasion. Just then, the back door opened, and two men emerged carrying heavy-looking trash containers... which they lifted and dumped on top of Sonya's things.

It was only ten-thirty, so she jogged slowly toward the apartment until she got herself under control. She slowed, walked and allowed her heartbeat to come back to somewhere near normal. She felt a great wave of satisfaction sweep over herself, knowing that she did great damage to Crummy Keller, but didn't manage to kill him. He would probably never walk again without pain and a limp. He would never know that it was his daughter who broke his body with such relative ease. He wouldn't be able to inflict anymore beatings on anyone for a long time. If he persisted in harassing and attacking her mother, she knew she would have to finish the job of defending her - and so many others - from the scourge and true evil of Crummy Keller.

When Sonya got home, her mother was just getting ready to crawl into bed. "I'm gonna stay up for a little while and watch some TV, Mom. I'm not tired yet."

"Okay, baby. Sleep good. See you tomorrow."

Sonya found some brandy and poured herself three fingers of the brown liquid in a glass. She had to counter the adrenaline. She turned on the TV to a late-night comedy show and tried to escape into the inanities of tonight's guest stars. The brandy and the babble eventually did their work. Sonya dragged herself into the bedroom and peeled off her "work" clothes. She did have the presence of mind to check them for blood spatters. There were none, but she dumped everything into the clothes washer and started it on anyway. The hot shower felt wonderful as the cascades drained her stress and excitement down the drain along with the soapy rivulets. It was then that she realized she had absolutely no remorse for her actions this evening. She just kept hearing that voice in her head that said, "The bastard deserved it!" There was no other self-talk commentary. Good.

Lights out. Time for sleep and recovery.

Chapter 5

LEARNING THE TAO

ERICA KELLER AWOKE THE NEXT morning to discover Sonya still asleep. She drank her coffee and headed out to work. It was another very cold winter day in Indiana and the forecast was for a new cold front with lots of snow to arrive sometime late that afternoon. While driving to work in her battered old blue Toyota, she listened to the morning news on the radio. It included a report of a man found in the town park who had been badly beaten. He was also a known felon and police suspected it was a drug deal gone wrong. The police spokesman said he was armed but looked like he'd been hit by a truck. There were several broken bones, a concussion and deep abdominal injuries. He just might live.

A reporter asked what the victim's name was. "Cromwell Keller," he said.

Erica jerked her head toward the radio and pulled over to listen to the rest of the report, but nothing more came of it. "Holy crap! Somebody beat Crummy half to death. It wouldn't surprise me that one of his turd-like pals worked him over because he hadn't paid for his latest drug buy," she said out loud. After a shoulder shrug and a smirk, Erica pulled back into traffic and went to work. The sky had just gotten a little brighter.

Sonya rolled out of bed about an hour after Erica left and heard her cell-phone buzzing. It was Kelsey. "Did you hear the news? Somebody kicked the shit out of Crummy and nearly killed him."

"No, I just woke up. What happened?"

"It happened last night, so it didn't make the papers, but the local TV news said that he had a broken jaw, elbow and ribs. One of his knees is ruined. The attacker or attackers even broke one of his ankles and dislocated a shoulder. Somebody really fucked him up."

"Oh. Wow! So, he lived?"

"Yeah, but just barely. The cops presented a front of 'good riddance' during the press conference."

"Well, I couldn't agree more. He really is a piece of shit and is dangerous to everyone he touches. I watched first-hand as the drugs turned his brain into that of a cave-dwelling monster. Good riddance indeed. Kelsey, I'm going over to the *do-jo* to talk to your father about a job. I'll call you later."

As she came out of her apartment, two uniformed police officers were just coming up the stairs. "What are you guys looking for?" she asked.

"We're looking for Erica and Sonya Keller. Know them?"

"I'm Sonya. My mom's at work. What can I do for you?"

"Well, your father just had the crap beaten out of him and there are a couple of complaints and criminal charges against him from you and your mother about assault and rape. Where were you last night?"

"I visited my friend Kelsey Morrow for a while."

"What time did you leave Kelsey's house?"

"About nine-thirty. Why?"

"Well, your father's attack occurred around ten or ten thirty. We're just covering all the bases."

"Okay. Well, I took a run after I left Kelsey's. I do that. In fact, I'm just headed over to my friend's studio for a workout. I ended up getting home a little before eleven, I think."

"That's quite a run."

"Yeah. I do a minimum of 5 miles. Since it's so cold, I don't run too fast and suck a lot of cold air into my lungs. So, last night it took a little over an hour to do the 5 miles."

"Is there anyone who can verify that you were on the run?"

"I don't think so. I usually try to find quiet streets at night so I won't have to dodge traffic or people."

"Okay. Well, it looks like your father was involved with drugs again. He had a pistol, but never got a chance to use it. He got broken up pretty bad. Anyway, he'll be off the streets for a long time and that's a good thing. A convicted felon possessing a firearm blows up his parole, so whenever he gets out of the hospital, he's going back to prison for who knows how long. Cromwell Keller is a very bad dude, but then you already know that. We're glad to see him out of circulation for a long time. I'm sure you two are too."

Without blinking, Sonya thanked the officers and walked over to the sidewalk where she started stretching before her run over to see Ned. Again, she didn't feel the slightest twinge of remorse or guilt from the lies she just told the police. Crummy and his pals had altered her conscience and her sense of right and wrong in terms of equivalent justice; she realized that she had become someone totally committed to eliminating the bad people wherever she found them... and felt no empathy whatsoever for their fates. They certainly felt no compassion or empathy for *their* victims. She knew her moral compass had shifted dramatically such that she now saw it having a kind of red zone where she felt her normal sweetness simply didn't have a place. The tables were about to turn on those who marketed in evil.

Sonya arrived at the *do-jo* and waited for Ned to finish a therapy session with one of his more muscular clients. When that session finished, he walked over and hugged his sort-of daughter. "I need a job, Ned. Can I help you teach classes?"

"Really? You want to do this?"

"Yes. It will give me a good excuse to keep in shape and learn more stuff.

Thanks again for the *daisho*. Now, I want to take *kendo* lessons and learn more of the *Tao*."

Ned smiled and said, "Well, grasshopper, we can do that. I've got a friend in Chicago who is a great *kendo* instructor and will advance your knowledge. Hell, you may even become a Buddhist if you're not careful."

"Oh, I doubt that. I don't have time in my life or room in my mind for religion. I just want to learn to never be weak or allow myself to be dominated by anything or anybody. So, when can we go to the rifle range?"

"You sure are anxious to be a *ninja,* aren't you?" he said, laughing. Sonya didn't laugh. That unnerving, steely glare once again appeared in her eyes.

"You know what I want. I'm not going to join the military. Too many rules. I want to make my own rules, but first I have to learn the elements of the game. Will you hire me, or will I have to look somewhere else? I love you and your family, of course, and I want to keep being part of it."

"No problem, my dear Sonya. You can conduct beginners' classes on personal defense. You've seen enough of them and have played a major role when you participated, so I think you'll do fine. I've got six new students, all women, coming in later this afternoon." He walked over to a desk and pulled out a prospectus for the course. "Read this and be here early – around four – to stretch and warm up. You'll be doing a lot of demonstrating at first and it wouldn't be good for you to pull a muscle, now would it?" He also pulled out the required W-4 IRS forms. She was now an official employee. The pay would be enough for her to split the rent with her mother with a little extra for herself.

Sonya was a little nervous with her first class, but after she stretched everybody out, she went through some of the basic escape moves using all six of the new class' students as "dummies". She then instructed each of them to try the moves on each other in a step-by-step manner until they could do them without thinking. At the end of class, everyone was sweating freely. Sonya told them all to take a good shower and towel completely dry before venturing out into the cold afternoon. "We can't afford having any frozen *ninjas,* now can we?" she quipped.

On one cool, sunny day a month later, with Kelsey home from college, the two women took a basketball down to the court behind their old elementary school. The red-brick walls and the peeling paint on the window frames reminded them both of those early, formative years. Seeing the old building gave them both a sense of transition from those halcyon days of childhood to their expanding adulthood. The paint around the window frames was peeling badly giving the building a kind of aged, sad look.

There was a three-on-three game going on using the full court. The old court had been patched many times, and the surface was uneven; players had to know the quirks if they wanted to keep the ball from bouncing out of their control. The women sat on the bench at court side and watched the young men play what looked like a pretty good game. There was a lot of running, fast breaks, quick passes and decent shooting and rebounding. After 15 minutes, two of the guys from one team stopped playing and retrieved their jackets. They had to go to job interviews requiring that they clean up. The four other players looked at Kelsey and Sonya and finally asked if they wanted to play.

"Sure," Kelsey said. "I play with a college freshman team, and my friend here has some game too. I taught her everything she knows, she dead-panned."

"Okay," one of the taller players said. "I'll take you two and play against those three guys. Oh. I'm Derek. That tall, brown drink of water is Shawn. The other two guys are Eddie and Joey. Are you two ready to play, or do you need to warm up?"

"We're good to go. I'm Kelsey and this is Sonya."

Derek threw the ball to Shawn for the take out and walked over to guard him. Kelsey covered Eddie, a white kid with wild, unkempt hair who was about her height at five-nine. That left Sonya on Joey, a dark-toned, handsome lad just over 6 feet. Shawn threw the ball in and the game began. They played fairly evenly for the first several minutes with the Joey/Eddie/Shawn team holding a slight edge. The game was speedy and both women had to scramble to keep pace with the talented men.

Kelsey made a silent gesture to Sonya and she whispered to Derek to throw a deep, lob pass to her when she took off on a fast break. After taking the inbounds pass from Kelsey, Derek dribbled a couple times in place and Sonya took off. Derek lobbed the ball to Sonya as she blew past Joey. She caught it, dribbled once and leaped for a backboard-rattling slam dunk.

Everyone but Kelsey stopped and stared in amazement. Kelsey tried to hide her grin and chuckles as she casually trotted back to her defensive position. "What? You never saw a girl dunk before?" was Sonya's retort. Derek, like the other three men stood there with mouths agape. He couldn't believe a girl could move like that. Kelsey said, off-handedly, "She does that all the time."

The opposing team started bringing the ball back up the court. At half-court, Sonya darted in and stole the ball from Joey and repeated her slam dunk performance, but with two hands this time. Derek and Kelsey gave high fives to Sonya, while the other team just looked at each other in amazement and shock. Another two-handed, behind the head slammer finished the game.

Without another try to bring the ball up the court, the three young men on the opposing team decided to call it a day. They shook hands all around and told Sonya they'd never seen a boy her size do what she did, never mind a girl. "I've been working out a lot," was Sonya's response. The boys just nodded and walked away. Derek gave high-fives to both girls.

"Kelsey, you have a great jumper. But YOU, Sonya... Man, I've never seen anyone that fast or able to jump like that. How tall are you?"

"Five-eleven and a little bit."

"I don't see guys take that much air. You're amazing. I'll pick you for my team anytime."

"Thanks, Derek. Why don't you come to my friend's *do-jo* sometime and learn something new?"

"Where is it? What's it called?"

"It's called *The Midwest Martial Arts and Self-Defense Studio.* It's over on Melrose in that little mini-mall."

"I know where it is. See you there sometime."

"Okay. I work there in the afternoons after three."

The women walked back to Kelsey's house laughing and joking about their basketball experience. "You really shouldn't show off like that, Sonya. It calls attention to yourself and I'd be afraid that the word would get around. Maybe you should be more careful."

"That Derek was kinda cute. Maybe I'll get to know him some."

Derek Murphy was 2 inches over 6 feet tall with skin the color of varnished oak. His eyes were bright green. His hair was of medium length and loosely curled; he was obviously the product of mixed-race parents.

"I know you're right, Kelsey, but I can't be a hermit, can I? I have you and who else as a friend? Ned and Evelyn, of course, but that's it. My mother worries about me in that way too. I've got to find a way to make more friends without fearing retribution from Crummy's drug pals. I know I can defend myself from assault, but what if they start shooting at me? I feel that gnawing fear every day when I go out. Someday, it will go away, and maybe I'll have to do things to make it go away. I worry about my mother being vulnerable to those motherfuckers too. I'm going to take those *kendo* lessons and learn how to become invisible when I'm out and about. Ned says it's the *Shinobi,* the way of the secret warrior. Maybe that's what I'll become: a secret warrior, the vanquisher of really bad people and the defender of the innocent against the demons all around us."

After a pause, they both looked at each other and laughed. But Sonya felt her own laugh was a bit hollow. Maybe she indeed needed to become a warrior for the sake of innocent people and children being chewed up and spat out by the wretched drug culture that was so deep and wide... even in this small town.

Erica had recently purchased another used Toyota for Sonya. It was nondescript gray, something that would become part of her warrior woman "equipment". Sonya's first visit to MOCOM (M- Martial Arts; O- Opacity; C- Camouflage; O- Operational; M- Mentality) Studios in Chicago was very enlightening and made her realize that there was much more to martial arts than breaking boards, throwing people through the air and, in her case, breaking bones. She noticed a big sign on the wall as she entered: *If you cannot detach yourself from death, then you will fear everything. It is said that nothing is a greater change than your own death: think on this. This is the same as stopping breathing for fear of aging.* - Heika Jodan, Issui-sensei, 1670.

She met Kyle Nelson before his first classes started. They discussed her motives, the curriculum that MOCOM offered and what sort of "warrior princess" she wanted to become. Nelson meant that last label in a joking fashion, but Sonya didn't laugh. In her mind, it was exactly what she wanted to be.

Kyle Nelson was a highly respected teacher and master of the arts of self-defense... *and* offense. Perfect. The large number of photos and certificates on his ego wall were impressive. Nelson stood about 5 feet 10 inches, shorter than Sonya, but was built like a cinder block, square and well-chiseled. He appeared to be in his early fifties with a lot of gray hair sprinkled through the jet black. He gave Sonya a brief background including that his mother was Japanese and a distant ancestor of one of the last real Samurai warriors of the eighteenth century. His father was an American naval officer who spent many years in Japan, meeting his mother, marrying her and bringing both of them back to the United States, years later, whereupon he retired. Kyle was his parents' only child and was raised more Japanese than American as his father was so often at sea. His mother, Hiroki, sent him to Japanese schools in Japan, of course, and where she could find them in America. It was in those schools where he met those connections that helped him begin learning the way of the warrior at an early age. Kyle was, of course, bi-lingual and taught special, advanced classes in Japanese at a local junior college. He told Sonya that if she signed up for his *kendo* and urban stealth classes, she would have to learn the Japanese lexicon for those classes. *Sensei* Nelson's last questions stopped Sonya in her tracks: "Why are you so interested in learning these skills? What do you hope to gain? You're a very attractive young woman and, from what Ned tells me, very smart. If your work here – and at Ned's place – is to be really worthy of the artistry, science and effort, you should have an operating philosophy. Have you thought of one?"

"Not really."

"Well, spend some time trying to define one. Start writing your thoughts and ideas focused on what we're going to do here."

There was little doubt in Sonya's mind that she would start his classes as soon as possible. She would drive into Chicago in the mornings and teach at Ned's *do-jo* in the afternoons. Perfect. On the drive home that first day, Sonya pondered *Sensei Nelson's* questions and realized that the only thing she'd come up with so far was venting her pain and rage on really bad guys. That was pure vigilante justice, but, she realized, it had no altruistic component; she wasn't helping or fixing anything but merely satisfying her own personal vendettas against the faceless foes who would do her and her loved ones harm. *Sensei* Nelson was right. She needed to develop a more mature, in-depth operating philosophy for what she was about to do. She had to face her fears, hate and anger. She already knew that a fighter filled with anger and hate was subjected to large adrenaline dumps which narrowed his or her field of vision and impeded quick, agile and subtle movement. In unsanctioned personal combat, those limiting factors could be lethal. She knew, then, that she had to learn the true meaning of the *Tao.*

During her next visit with *Sensei* Nelson, he waxed into the philosophy of the Taoist myths of creation and what *yin* and *yang* actually meant to the true believer. *Yin* and *Yang* translate into earth and heaven. Man is embedded in this dichotomy. When the body dies, *yin* and *yang* separate: *yin,* the body, crumbles and returns to earth. *Yang,* the spirit, returns to heaven. Therefore, death is not an end but the beginning of another phase of life. Understanding this allows the *shinobi* to face death without fear.

SO, WHERE DOES MY PAIN fit in with all this, she thought? *Was my violation enough to justify my desire to seek vengeance against those who did us harm? What about the inherent dangers of drugs in our society? Even my best friend was attacked by kids seeking money for drugs. What is so fucking important about being high? Is everyone in so much pain they need to be numbed to it? Or are they so bored that getting high sets their minds free to... do what? What does a "freed mind" of a druggie really do? Where does it go? Is it the hallucinations for escape? Why do they feel the need to escape? From what? Are their lives so miserable that the only way to escape is through chemicals that will eventually destroy them or turn their brains to mush? What good to society are they? Why should they be allowed to reproduce? What will their drugged-out offspring be like? Won't they be more of a burden on society? Who pays for these drooling losers holed up in some stinking, leaky, rat-infested apartment or shack? The law doesn't seem to be able to quell or slow this rampant drug-oriented society. Why not? Is there too much money in it and everyone is on the take? Why don't our elected officials actually DO something? How do the drug lords get away with it all the time? What's wrong with our system that this drug money seems to run the show? I know that some of the richest Latin American drug lords actually spread the wealth to their followers and thus create a supporting force of thousands. They are like mother's milk to the people caught up in the abject poverty of those poor countries. But the lords also expect payment from them in the form of being "mules" for trafficking and bodyguards to protect them. I've read horror stories about whole families being killed because they wouldn't become employees of the drug cartels. No wonder we have so many people running for their lives coming to our southern border.*

But we're not a poor country, are we? In fact, from what I've read, our available, discretionary money is enough to actually run the entire economy of the poorest Central American countries where these major drug makers and traffickers live. What did I read? Five BILLION dollars a year our drug-addled fools give away to these "lords". For what? Do our American drug users actually feel good about feeding and housing people in Honduras? I doubt it. They are so self-centered, self-indulgent and self-absorbed that anybody or anything outside of their immediate needs doesn't matter. Otherwise, why would they attack innocent people like Kelsey for money to get high?

After rolling all this around in her mind on the drive home, Sonya arrived at Ned's *do-jo* to lead the next class in self-defense. She barely said "hi" to Ned as the thoughts from her drive back from Chicago kept swirling.

Chapter 6

LEARNING TO BE GRAY

WHAT THE HECK DID BEING "gray" mean? She set about learning the new terminology and the philosophy in combination from the ancient Chinese/Japanese cultures to the more modern, Cold War generated meaning behind the skills and overall philosophy of the stealthy warrior. Sonya's first lessons at MOCOM Studios were written – and lengthy. She spent the 2 hours there reading a thick booklet and was only half done when she had to leave. Her first new words were *shinobi no mono,* literally meaning "hiding person". The associated skills with *ninjutsu,* or *shinobi no jutsu* means "the arts of the *shinobi,* or the arts belonging to the *shinobi* warrior – more prosaically known as a *ninja.* One of those arts was being invisible in several environments including being unseen in plain sight.

As Sonya continued to read, she gained one of the most important aspects of "being gray": *situational awareness.* This mental discipline is what keeps fighter pilots alive in the combat zone. It is how the police, the FBI and the CIA school their people to help keep them alive in high danger situations. She learned that being unaware allows for "flight or fight" body mechanisms to dump adrenaline into one's system, thus limiting field of vision and fine, subtle movements that might be just enough to survive or be the victor in an encounter with an opponent. Athletes often call this "maintaining your cool".

She also learned about dressing in public to avoid standing out in a crowd of *any* size. Outgoing behavior, emotional outbursts and loud speech were also anathema to being unseen in plain sight. Kelsey's comment about exhibiting her prowess on the basketball court came to mind.

The readings triggered more emotional responses than she thought they would, and that in itself spelled *caution. Don't get all wrapped up in your self-assigned mission so that you lose sight of how you're going to accomplish it and survive.* She remembered her first mission against Crummy and was pleased that she did so many things right according to the *shinobi.* Ned must have had this kind of training too when he was a SEAL. Ned was her mentor and next-best friend. She wanted to honor that relationship and his teachings. A new level of focus and mental discipline would now be part of her life. She also realized, that in her growing maturity, she would not let the discipline of the *Tao* ruin who she was as a person nor her personality. There were many things on Sonya's agenda that were part of her maturation and personal change... for better or worse.

In the next visits, Nelson worked Sonya out and sparred a little. He was highly impressed with her physical attributes, her speed, skills and technique. Ned had taught her well. He also saw that what Ned *didn't* teach her was the intensity with which Sonya expressed herself both in physical training and sparring. Her power transcended the physical; she was like a racehorse at the bell. Nelson felt that he had to have discussions about her craft of martial arts and the mental aspects of controlling it.

"You are a powerful young thing, Sonya Keller," he began. "But you have some maturation to gain. Even in your beginner lessons you exhibit a kind of intensity that is very rare. You are, obviously, very powerful, but it's the focus and intensity that set you apart from virtually every student. The thing is you *must* understand what power is. What I mean is that your power must be checked from time-to-time. You can't just peg the needle with every blow, punch or maneuver. You must learn and know the degree of power required for each situation. I know Ned is teaching you to use firearms. He tells me that you're already a natural marksman. That, too, is not surprising considering how your intensity and focus work for you on the mats. So, what I'm trying to point you toward is knowing when to focus absolutely and when to use your maximum power as situations dictate. That's the true meaning of *situational awareness."*

"I think I understand. Ned tells me I'm stronger and faster than most men, but I don't know where it came from. It just happened when I started working out and running. So, are you saying, *Sensei,* that I must learn to not maximize my strength and power every time?"

"Yes. That's precisely what I mean. I don't know what you have in mind beyond the gym or the *do-jo,* but understand that if you're in a real-life combat situation, you may find that maximizing your effort may leave you vulnerable to counter-attack, or make you overshoot your target, or do more harm to your attacker than is legally allowable... if you get my meaning?"

"Oh. I hadn't thought about any of those things. I just felt I had to go all-out every time."

"Ned told me a little about your history. Don't worry, he was very discreet."

"So, you know that my father beat my mother and allowed his drug friends to rape my mother and me?"

"No. I didn't know that. My god! Is that where your fury comes from?"

"Yes. Every opponent or every punching bag or every board looks like them."

"I had no idea it was that bad. I'm so sorry."

"Thanks for that, but I made a vow to never be so weak and vulnerable again, and I want to be able to protect my mother should those bastards come back. If they do, I will break every bone in their fucking bodies!"

Ned's neck hair started to bristle as he felt the anger and the raw emotion radiate out from Sonya as if she was an atomic reactor. "Then, my little lecture to you about knowing what power is and how to use it was more appropriate than I imagined. I can see your motivation, but, more than ever, I'd hate to see you do something you'd regret."

"Why do you think I'm doing all this stuff, *Sensei?* It isn't me who is going to do the regretting. Three kids attacked my best friend to steal her money to buy drugs. The court system basically let them off with a light jail sentence. I just can't let punks and criminals like that be allowed to keep hurting people, especially my friends and family. Drugs have always been part of every society in all of history, I learned. Okay, I get that. But the criminal enterprises that market and run drugs to our children must be injured. Somehow, I intend to do some of that injuring even if it's just local."

By now, Nelson could feel the heat in the room as he watched Sonya become increasingly passionate from the kettle of anger, shame and frustration she kept on the boil. He wondered if what he was teaching Sonya could come back to harm himself as an accessory to any crimes she might commit. Sensing that, Sonya said, "Don't worry, *Sensei.* Nobody knows I'm doing this except you and Ned. Ned and his family aren't going to say anything about anything no matter what. They know what happened when they took me in the very night I was raped and escaped out the bedroom window. They understand my anger and what I feel is my sense of duty. I know I have special physical attributes, but I want to be under control so I DON'T do anything that will get me or anybody else in trouble. We're the good guys. The 'good guys' don't get sent to jail. That's also why your lessons are so valuable to me."

Nelson decided it was time to teach her the basic moves of *kendo* using the bamboo *katana.* This "sword" was made of stout bamboo, usually, and was shaped like the metal fighting swords, or *katana* of *samurai* legend. The fighters in *kendo* wore protective gear and masks to prevent serious injury. Still, a spirited match could yield significant bruising. Footwork, balance and aggressiveness all had to operate in a balanced way to serve the fighter both on offense and defense. After these emotionally revealing discussions, they both needed to expel some tension and burn off the excess energy. After donning the protective gear, Nelson showed Sonya the basic positions and technique for balance as well as attacking with strength. Attacks are not subtle and defense against them is very difficult. After an hour of basics and some freewheeling, both Sonya and Nelson were dripping with sweat and breathing heavily.

"For a first-time 'warrior', you were very good. Your aggressive nature will make you a very formidable opponent someday. I didn't bruise you too badly, did I?" Nelson asked smiling.

"Not bad. I'll heal. Did I get any hits on you?"

"Oh yes, and I felt your power. When you master more technique, you will overpower most of your opponents, male or female. Well, there aren't too many female *kendo* fighters. Where did you get all that strength?"

"Ned let me use his weight room whenever I wanted. After I escaped Crummy and friends, my mom went to live in a shelter, and I stayed with the Morrows. I was just seventeen, so I'm now like their other daughter. My mom found an apartment and I live there most of the time. I feel I need to be near her for protection. All these things added up, I guess, and I worked really hard. When I started running a lot, I found that I could run *fast* for long distances... and short ones too. Ned says I have world-class speed. I can dunk a basketball with two hands and high jump over most fences. Once I made my muscles strong, I found I could do some amazing things... or so Ned says."

Nelson listened to this intensely and handed Sonya another book on stealth and warrior skills. Behind each skill, he noted, there is an operating philosophy and she should acquire that philosophy to enhance her specific and overall skill suite. Having so much mental strength enhanced the physical strength and made mission accomplishments much more likely to succeed.

Learning to be "gray" and wearing appropriate clothing for every part of every day was critical. Nelson told Sonya to forget all the movie stereotypes about ninja warriors. First, she was not answering to any "Lord". She was her own boss. Second, most of the ancient weapons didn't really apply anymore, not with guns and explosives being so prevalent. Oh, there was a place for the swords, the blowguns, the bows and arrows and the hand-to-hand stuff, but the time for glorifying them had passed. Urban camouflage technology was as simple as wearing colors and patterns matching the surroundings including some Canadian-designed wear that had vertical and horizontal lines and differently shaded panels to emulate walls of buildings. Black was mostly replaced with shades of gray that tended to match the very low light of shadows in alleys and such, hence the term "being gray".

Nelson schooled Sonya in all this information and taught her furtive movement through low and high light environments. He even gave her a lecture and demonstration about how our Native Americans had perfected stealth movement and guerrilla warfare long before Europeans came to North America.

"Here again, focusing on micro-movement was the key: feel every pebble with your foot. Anticipate a twig or leaf before you put down your foot. Put your foot down in sections: heel, instep, then roll your toes down starting with the small toe. One practicing this technique can be virtually silent in almost any setting."

Sensei also noted that this stealthy movement discipline melded perfectly with the Japanese-based code of the warrior, *Bushido*. Nelson drilled her on these techniques and Sonya practiced stealth movement using twigs and even cornflakes just to minimize noise making. Sonya soon realized that her physical conditioning was very important to keep her muscles in control rather than have them tremble or twitch from fatigue.

Sensei Nelson was happy and proud to see Sonya rapidly becoming a "gray" princess warrior, something she only imagined becoming just a few months ago. *Sensei* Nelson and Ned Morrow were her "masters" to her "grasshopper". As with Ned Morrow, Kyle Nelson took Sonya under his wing as his *kohai*, or favored student. In a few months, both Morrow and Nelson held a little ceremony for Sonya. Only Kelsey was allowed to attend. The two martial arts teachers invoked their blessings on Sonya admitting that they had no more to teach her. They had shown her the ways to keep improving every skill, every discipline, every training method and every mental aspect of the martial arts. She was now on her own.

Chapter 7

THE SECOND MISSION

DURING THE SUMMER OF HER twenty-first year, Sonya moved up to teaching more advanced classes at Ned's *do-jo*. She also worked and studied very hard to become more skilled and accomplished in *kendo*. Kyle Nelson sponsored her in an all-city *kendo* competition in Chicago that same summer. She was the only female contestant but dressed and carried herself such that her gender was unknown to anyone else. She became "Sandy" Keller.

In one very spirited and competitive match, "Sandy" broke two katanas hitting her opponents with such great force. In one of the bouts, her blows knocked her opponent down and a referee had to step in to prevent "Sandy" from continuing the assault. A kind of rustling hush fell over the audience while watching her matches. In her next match, she once again displayed uncommon strength by breaking her opponent's *katana* but kept swinging hers. Once again, a referee had to step in, but this time the officiating committee disqualified "Sandy" as being too undisciplined even for the violent sport of *kendo*.

On the drive back to Nelson's studio, *Sensei* admonished Sonya severely for failing to control her emotions and her force. "I told you and told you about knowing your power and how and when to use it. Why did you lose control?"

"I don't know. I just felt my demons come through. I couldn't stop them. It was like I was transformed into something else. I once read about a Hindu goddess named Durga. She had ten arms, each one holding a different weapon given to her by the gods. As Shiva's consort, her job was to protect the innocent and destroy the demons that plagued the world. Somehow, I feel like I have ten arms and want to slay every demon out there. Maybe I need to go to anger management to sort this out. Is my aggression part of a kind of PTSD that I've read about from soldiers and victims of violence have to deal with?"

"You damn near injured the defending champion, Sonya. What drives you is beyond anything more I can teach you. I'm not sure I can help you anymore. You're going to have to get a grip on your own power and emotions. If you don't, someone is going to pay a severe price for it, and that someone might be you. Yes. I would recommend you get some anger management help."

They rode the rest of the way in silence. Nelson helped Sonya unload her equipment and load it into the back of her car. He shook her hand, wished her the best and walked into the studio without offering her any tea or further conversation.

On her drive home, Sonya began to realize that she had crossed another line, another segment of her life. She knew now that she was on her own with her talent, her power, her skill and, above all else, her state of mind. The rage and anger she harbored still seethed like a constant hurricane waiting for the right conditions to burst forth and wreak havoc on her foes. Her mission-oriented attitude hadn't changed, but the fact that she had pushed away a real expert because of her rage made her feel a little frightened, sad and, at the same time, somehow elated. Once the realization came to her that she was more than just a special talent, but rather, an extraordinary being destined to do extraordinary things within and without the formal and legal system of justice, she felt a humbling emotion sweep over her that troubled her sense of being and her understanding of right versus wrong. Tears flooded her eyes so that she had to pull over and let the emotions pour out of herself. She sobbed for several minutes. It was the sense of loss from *Sensei* Nelson's admonishment and the realization that she still allowed the horror of her past to drive her life.

She wondered and pondered what her next mission would be. Shortly after she got home, her phone rang.

It was Kelsey. "One of the kids who jumped me 2 years ago stopped me on the street again and threatened me if I didn't give him a thousand dollars. I was just walking back home from the grocery store at the corner and he popped out from between two buildings. He had a knife. He didn't make an aggressive move with it, just played with it in front of my eyes."

"Okay. Did he give you some contact information? Where and when were you to meet him?"

"He said to meet him in the corner field next to the schoolyard behind the elementary school at eight o'clock tomorrow night. What am I going to do?"

"Did you agree to meet him? What were his threats?"

"I said yes, because he took a step closer and held the knife up. He said he'd cut me up like a jigsaw puzzle if I didn't pay. He said that he had to spend 6 months in juvenile prison because of me. I just wasn't in position to take his weapon."

"Well, we'll just have to meet this guy. I wonder if he'll come alone or bring his pals. I'm coming with you."

"Oh, I was hoping you'd say that. I didn't tell my parents because I didn't want to worry them."

"Well, we'll take care of all the worry. I'll come over about seven tomorrow. I'll come straight from the *do-jo*. This will be interesting. Nobody assaults my friend with a weapon. He's not gonna like the outcome."

The next day at work, Sonya finished teaching her last class and went to her locker to dress in her "combat" clothes. It was a warm evening, so she wore only the yoga suit with a strong, wide sash. She stuffed the *daisho* into the sash with the *katana on* the left side so she could draw it with her right, or strongest hand. The *wakizashi* she tucked into the right side of the sash. Over this, she wrapped a gray-colored, lightweight, silk robe that effectively hid her swords. She looked at herself in the mirror and was pleased that the scabbards didn't show. Next, she wrapped a large matching gray bandana around her head so that only her face showed. She put on another similar bandana around her neck, like in Western movies, so that she could pull it up to cover everything but her eyes.

SHE REMOVED THE SWORDS AND drove over to Kelsey's house. As they drove to the meeting, Sonya told Kelsey her plan. They scouted the meeting area and saw no CCTV cameras anywhere. The corner field was shaded by large elms. Good. The evening light and shadows would be just right at eight o'clock for a stealthy setup. They parked about 80 meters from the park with a clear field of view. Sonya told Kelsey to flash her hand-held phone light just once when she recognized the threat maker. When Sonya rendered a hand signal, Kelsey was to call the police and start the car. Sonya would become "gray" among the elms. They'd never see her until she wanted them to. Also, since Kelsey was known to these punks, she wouldn't be anywhere near the "meeting". The punks wouldn't know Sonya in broad daylight let alone in her "combat" garb. They'd never seen her before.

Sonya, swords in hand, walked through shadows to the park and moved slowly and carefully among the trees imagining herself to be a wraith as she took her hiding place just off a small clearing in the copse of trees. She kept the sun behind her, positioning the two swords in her sash. She waited. Just after eight o'clock three young men came into the park from an adjacent street entrance; the park being bordered by a low, knee-high fence. One of the men was wearing a hooded sweatshirt even though it was close to ninety sultry degrees. Another wore a simple, black T-shirt with a backwards ball cap. The third man was wearing a long-sleeved blue T-shirt. The three slunk into the clearing looking around.

When they were within a few feet of Sonya's position, they clearly still hadn't seen her.

"Are you gentlemen looking for someone?" Sonya spoke in her lowest voice register.

"Who the fuck are you?" They still couldn't see her even knowing the direction from which her voice emitted.

"I'm just a friend. What do you guys want?" Sonya said as she stepped out where they could see her silhouette.

"WHERE'S THAT NIGGER GIRL? SHE'S gonna pay us our money. She owes us for being in that fucking county jail."

"I'm afraid she's not here tonight, but I am." Sonya stepped out into the clearing where the three hoodlums could see her. Her striking presence and covered face made them jump back and pull out their knives. No guns. Good.

"Are you gonna give us our money or do we have to cut you up too?"

The "hoody" took a step forward indicating that he was the leader of these three.

"No, I'm not going to give you any money."

"Okay, then I guess we'll have to cut you up." With that he lunged toward Sonya with his 8-inch hunting knife brandished in his right hand.

There was a quick, sharp hiss and a flash of steel catching the last rays of the setting sun. In the next instant, most of "hoody's" hand hit the grass with his knife still in it. Barely a heartbeat later, "backward cap" had a slash from shoulder to waist diagonally across his chest causing him to drop his weapon. By now, "hoody" was screaming in acute pain and "blue shirt" was frozen in place. Sonya swung her *katana* at blue shirt's neck, stopping at just the right time to give him a small nick on the side it. "Drop your knife or lose your head, asshole!"

"Blue shirt" snapped out of his trance, dropped his blade and took off toward the park's low fence. In his haste, he didn't see the fence and it caught him just below the knee sending him face-first onto the concrete sidewalk knocking him senseless.

Sonya turned back to the other two thugs and watched "backward cap" try to staunch his own wound while trying to wrap "hoody's" sliced hand with the sweatshirt. "So, the next time you mess with my friend, *boys,* you'll find yourselves dealing with me. You want to do drugs, then go do them. Rot your pathetic brains all you want, but you're not doing it on my time or that of my friend. Get it?" With that, Sonya waved to Kelsey.

They looked up with hate and fire in their eyes. Good. "Go call the cops and see what they think of two or three parolees being caught in an assault with deadly weapons. Oh, wait. They should be here any second. I think I hear the sirens now."

When the sirens indeed were audible, Sonya melted into the shadows once again and found her way back to the car while removing her headwear and rolling the swords up in her robe. As Kelsey pulled away from the curb, she looked at Sonya who still had her "game face" on. "Thanks, Sonya. I'm so grateful for you defending me against those bastards. If I'd told my father, he'd have probably killed them."

"If those three assholes ever bother you again, *I* will kill them. Three strokes, three heads on the street. Just like in the movies."

With that comment, followed by a brief pause, the two young women burst into hysterical laughter. Kelsey had to pull over while they got over their spasms of relief from the adrenaline and very dark humor. Nothing seals a friendship like an act of love, support and unqualified duty to that bond. Once again, the image of Durga emerged from Sonya's mental imagery. She hadn't exactly slain any demons, but she certainly defended the innocent against them. Or as Ned said from something one of his fellow SEALS kept saying, *If you fuck with my friends, my country or my loved ones, I will visit such force upon your sorry ass, that nobody will ever find all the pieces.*

When Sonya got home with her swords, she cleaned them with soap, water, alcohol and bleach, scrubbing every surface with a stiff brush. She then got out the special honing stone and re-sharpened the blade of her *katana*. It was a ritual taught to her by *Sensei* Nelson. It also removed any residual evidence from those catching the business end of the sword. The adrenaline still hadn't quite burned itself off, so Sonya's hands trembled slightly as she cleaned up. She stood in the shower rinsing away her amped up feelings until all the hot water was gone.

Chapter 8

A New Dimension

DEREK MURPHY WALKED INTO THE *do-jo* late one warm Tuesday afternoon, while Sonja was doing some paperwork. She looked up and did a double take. "Oh. Hi. Haven't seen you since the basketball game. How are you? It's been a few weeks. I'd totally forgotten about you; I've been so busy."

"I'm fine. I decided to take you up on your offer to see your workplace. Is this a real karate studio?"

"Yup, and a whole lot more. We teach self-defense as well as the true art part of martial arts. We'll do everything but make you a *samurai* warrior," she said, then grinned broadly. "What can I do for you?"

"Well, just show me around, I guess. I don't think I'm *samurai* material. Are you busy? Do you have a weight room?"

"I'm not too busy to show you around. Yes, we do have a small weight room for those folks – mostly women – who want to build their muscular strength a little. My boss is also a private trainer and works with pro athletes and the like; anybody who can afford his rates." They both laughed.

Sonya continued to teach classes at Ned's *do-jo*. He had turned more and more of his classes over to her while he concentrated more on his personal, private clients in professional sports or executives seeking his personal skills and care. This combination of businesses provided a very nice income, so he was able to pay Sonya better. She was now sharing the rent with her mother and even talked about getting a bigger place or finding one of her own. Erica also received some raises in pay too, and life became more comfortable for her and her daughter. Crummy had disappeared into the penal system, but she suspected that his pals, "Rooster", Jimmy and "Demon" were still lurking about and staying involved in the drug trade.

Sonya gave Derek the grand tour and returned to the main studio. "So, is this where you throw people around and break boards?"

"Yes. Do you want me to show you some moves? Everyone should really know some basics because you never know when some thug is going to attack you. Have you ever been attacked?"

Derek smiled and said, "Nah. I've always been big enough to not get anyone interested enough to get in my, er, stuff."

Sonya noticed the deep dimple on his right cheek when he smiled. He also had a shallow cleft in his chin. *Hmmm. I've never looked at a guy like this before.*

"So, Sonya, when do you get off work? I'd like to buy you a coffee."

"Oh. Uh. I'm done with lessons for the day, so all I have to do is put a few things away. Sure. That would be great." *Holy crap! I'm going on a date. I'm almost twenty-one years old and never been on a date. How the hell do I manage this? What if he tries to kiss me? I've never kissed ANYBODY.*

Sonya scurried about with trembling hands putting equipment back in the correct cabinet and putting a couple files back in their filing cupboard. She fumbled some and dropped some folders. She shot an apologetic glance over her shoulder and shrugged at Derek who smiled back appropriately. She grabbed her key chain and the light kimono she wore on this warm, early summer day. She locked up and Derek pointed toward his car. It was a nondescript foreign sedan with an uneven paint job. "This is my chariot, madam. Allow me to assist."

My god! He's actually holding the door open for me. I've only seen this in the movies. What are my lines supposed to be?

"Oh, thank you, kind sir." They both laughed at the affectation.

"I thought women just said that in the movies," Derek said.

Uh. That's where I learned it. I don't know anything about boys, dating or standard banter. I'm super dumb at everything. Maybe I've had my head down for too long. The trauma, the anger, the hate, the smell of men has made me kind of immune to anything they'd say, least of all someone who is showing an interest in me. Oh, shit. I'm going to make a fool of myself. Well, here goes...

Derek drove a couple blocks to a small coffee shop. Sonya was starving after skipping lunch and grabbed a sandwich off the cooler shelf. "Oh, so I get to feed you too? Let me call my accountant to see if I can afford you," he said, then grinned that distinctive grin.

"Oh. I, uh... Look, Derek, I have to confess that I've never been taken out anywhere without paying my own way. I know this is the way it's supposed to go between boys and girls, er, men and women, but I've never been in this situation for real. I've only seen it in movies."

Derek stared at her with a stunned look on his face. "You're kidding, right?"

"No, Derek, this is my first real date."

"What? A good-looking woman like you? Nobody's ever asked you out?"

"No, but to be honest I've never put myself in a place to be asked out... or even to meet boys or men socially. See, I was home-schooled for a couple years and just worked the rest of the time. I've been to a bunch of martial arts classes and belt competitions, but they were pretty intense, and I was too locked in to flirt... or whatever it is girls do. So, there wasn't much socializing at all. I'd just finish my classes or workouts, shower and head home. I live with my mother and we kind of look out for one another. She doesn't go out much either... maybe once or twice a month with the girls. Me? I just read, work out, run, watch old movies on TV and conduct these classes."

After a lengthy silence, Derek picked up the coffee from the barista and they found a table next to a window. "I'm not surprised that you're such a workout lady. I can't get your dunks out of my mind from that basketball game. Man! How did you learn to do that?"

"Uh, well it just sort of happened. I had some tough times as a kid, and I got tired of being just a weak string bean. When I met Kelsey's dad – you remember Kelsey from the game? – he started working me out and I started lifting and running. After about a year, I got to be really strong and really fast... at least according to Ned."

"How strong is strong? How fast is fast?"

After a pause she smiled at Derek for the first time and blushed. *Oh, shit. I'm blushing.* "Well I can do fifteen one-arm pull ups with each arm, bench two-seventy-five ten times and squat almost five-hundred. Is that good?"

Derek just stared at her and nodded dumbly. "I don't know anyone who can do that. Are you sure you're not a superhero and are sizing me up for a conquest?"

"Of course not, silly. I'm just Sonya Keller, girl karate teacher.

"Ned timed me a couple weeks ago in 100 meters at just under 11 seconds. My mile time is just over 4 minutes. I want to break that 4-minute barrier this year."

"Uh, that would be a world record, Sonya. No woman has ever run under 4 minutes. Power, speed, good looks and brains... You are the whole package. You also seem really nice. What did you do before you got so into your physical self?"

It was as if a dark cloud had passed over the sun. Sonya's eyes clouded up, her face pinched and the smile faded into a scowl. Her jaw muscles clenched and Derek could see the tension in her arms and hands increasing by the second.

"I'm sorry to pry. I didn't mean to cause you any upset."

After a few seconds, Sonya relaxed and just nodded. "I don't know you well enough to tell you my story. Suffice to say that it is, uh, dramatic. Tell me about yourself. I know absolutely nothing about you. I've never 'interviewed' a boy, er, man before. If I'm going to drink coffee with strange men, I should know a little about them, right?"

Derek began by telling her that his mother was a very pretty blonde woman who was also tall and athletic, but nothing like Sonya. His father was African-American and a "player" in Chicago.

"HE RAN AROUND WITH SHADY characters, gambled, chased women and otherwise tried to be the *man* about town. When I was ten, dad split for parts unknown and Mom moved back here, her hometown. She worked a couple jobs to keep us in rent and groceries but insisted that I study hard in school and get good grades. It paid off. I got a small basketball AND academic scholarship to the junior college in town. I just finished my 2-year degree in May, and I'm now looking for work."

All the time Derek recounted his life story, Sonya became fascinated with the green eyes and the dimples. She began to feel a stirring of actual affection and warmth toward this tall, engaging fellow. *Will he ask me out again, or should I ask him to do something together sometime? Hell, I don't know the protocol. I'll just ask him when the time is right.*

"So, would you like to go to a movie with me this weekend?" he asked.

Oh, good. I don't have to ask.

"Okay. What's good?"

"I'll have to look. Maybe the new *Star Wars* movie. Do you like science fiction?"

"I don't know. I don't think I've ever seen a movie like that."

"You never watched *Star Trek* on TV before?"

"No." She was starting to feel really inadequate at being so far removed from Derek's obvious experience even in TV programming. She realized that she never had the "normal" young person's life that he had – or anyone else, for that matter.

"Not to worry. You're gonna love it. Lots of action. Even some romance. Are you a "romance" girl?"

"Definitely not." More blushing.

"Let me have your phone number and I'll call with date and time after I look in the paper."

Since she'd never given out her phone number to anyone before, she didn't know how to do that. Derek, sensing her confusion, pulled a pad and a pen from his jacket and handed them over to her. She had to think a bit to remember her own number, having never called it before.

"Keller."

"My last name is Murphy. Yeah. I know. My mother defaulted to her family's name when we moved back here. My father's last name was Poindexter. You can see why it was easy to take on Murphy as our last name. Her parents and family accepted me right away and have been very supportive. Nobody is rich, but they help us out whenever they can. Good people. You'd like them, I think."

Sonya and Derek talked for a while longer, then he drove her back to her car. He shook her hand and smiled. She smiled back and thanked him for the sandwich and coffee. "Talk to you tomorrow or the next day," he said, and drove off.

Sonya sped home, and immediately called Kelsey. "Remember that guy Derek we played basketball with? He asked me to go to the movies this weekend. I said yes! What have I done?"

"It sounds like you did what any normal, healthy woman would do if a sexy guy asked her out."

"But what do I do? What do I wear? What if he tries to kiss me? HELP!"

"Not to worry, sister. He seems to be a good guy. Go with it. Those lowlifes who introduced you to men are the rarity. They are the scum of the Earth. I just don't see evil in Derek. Good for you! Wear anything appropriate for movies and maybe a drink afterwards. You're not twenty-one yet, so you can't drink alcohol. If he tries to get you to drink alcohol, drop him like a bad habit. How old is he?"

"I don't know. Around our age, I think."

"Does he work, or is he in school?"

"He said he just got his 2-year degree at the JC and is looking for a job."

"Uh, huh. Well, don't be afraid to pay for your half of the date. That's called 'Dutch treat'."

"Why am I so excited? After everything I've been through, why is this *date* thing so unnerving?"

"Well, my sister, you never really had a social life as a teenager. You've never been where you could meet guys that are worth a shit. You've just led a sheltered life. Heck, I'm just starting to date at Northwestern. It's a little nerve-wracking because I'm always waiting for something screwy to happen. Look, Sonya, you're a beautiful woman and certainly capable of taking care of yourself. Any guy worth anything will be at least attracted to you. But your problem is going to be to let yourself be yourself with guys you meet... and with women too. The worst thing any of us can do is to try to be somebody we think the other person wants to see. I've learned that always leads to a disastrous date or outing. I know it's easy to just say, 'be yourself', but that's it. To me, you are my sister, and I love you to pieces. I love who you are with me. Just pretend you're out with me... so to speak. You will, of course, call me immediately afterwards to give me the rundown. Hear?"

"Of course. Thanks for listening and giving me advice. I've gotta get dinner ready for Mom. Talk to you soon."

Sonya floated around the apartment trying to organize dinner for her and Erica. It didn't go well. When Erica got home, one look told her that Sonya was not her normal, organized self. "What happened?"

"That guy I played basketball with a couple months ago came into the *do-jo* as I was closing up and took me out for coffee. Then, he asked me to go to the movies with him on Saturday... I think. So, I'm a little weird right now. Today was my first date ever. I am worried that our next date will be a nightmare on the one hand, and on the other hand, Derek seems like a really nice guy... and he's cute as hell."

"Calm down. Let's call in pizza, because it looks like making dinner is too much for you tonight." With that, Erica called up the local pizzeria for a delivery. "So, Derek, is it? You had coffee with him today? What's he like? Tell me everything."

In a slightly scattered fashion, Sonya told her mother the details of their coffee date. "Well, he sounds like a very nice boy. I'm sure you know how to spot danger signals by now. Don't worry. Just be your own delightful self. It will bring out the best in Derek too. I'm very happy for you. You – WE have been through some serious shit the last couple years, so maybe we deserve something good happening. I'm still trying to work on my attitudes. I'm making friends at the office so maybe, someday soon, I can come home like an excited schoolgirl talking YOUR ear off about a hot date." They both laughed. The doorbell rang, and they opened it to the smell of pepperoni and sausage pizza. Erica even let Sonya drink a cold beer with the pizza as a kind of celebration. It felt a little like

a coming out for her daughter. Finally.

Chapter 9

DEREK & SONYA

DEREK DID CALL THE NEXT DAY and made a date with Sonya to see an action/adventure movie featuring both male and female heroic figures. He collected her on time and met Erica. Derek was all smiles and good manners. He wore clean, casual clothes and was freshly shaved. Sonya actually wore a loose-fitting, sleeveless dress that allowed her well-muscled arms to see the light of day. Derek drove them slowly to the theater, parked and actually started around the car to open Sonya's door, but she'd already vaulted out of her side. "Were you really going to open my door?" she asked.

"Well, yeah, but clearly I'm not fast enough for you." They both laughed and walked into the movie theater, bought popcorn and soft drinks and found their seats. They didn't speak much while munching and waiting for the cartoons and previews to finish. Finally, the main feature began with all the loudness and high-energy music designed to prepare the audience for the coming thrills, danger and heroics. Derek mentioned that their shoes might stick to the floor from dropped candy.

"So be careful when you lift your foot that you don't come out of your shoes," he joked.

There were some tense action moments in the film when Sonya actually reached out and grabbed Derek's hand. He didn't let it go, and she didn't pull back. They shared shy smiles and watched the rest of the film as so many boys and girls, men and women did: holding hands. *This dating thing isn't so bad. I think I like this guy. He has large, strong hands too.*

Derek also had his own private thoughts and did some self-talk. *This woman is BEAUTIFUL and strong and very nice. I wonder why she doesn't already have boyfriends circling the block. Those callouses on her hands must come from the weights she lifts. I'm glad she didn't squeeze too hard. Easy does it, boy. I wonder if she knows enough to send the appropriate signals when the time is right. Do NOT push anything with this girl. She is clearly something special.*

The movie ended and the couple walked back toward the car once again holding hands. Sonya looked into Derek's bright green eyes and smiled. She didn't smile often, and it felt so natural to do so this time. Derek smiled back, of course. Sonya's dimples were as irresistible to Derek as his own were to her. "Let's go have some ice cream," he said.

"Great idea. Louie's down the street is pretty good."

"Oh, so you know the ice cream parlors, do you?"

"You bet. I don't get too many sweet treats, so when I get the chance I go for the best."

They both laughed. "Next thing you know, we'll be going to places that have cloth napkins," he said.

"Are you saying we should have another date?"

"That's exactly what I'm saying." Grin.

Louie's was almost full on this Saturday night, and Derek found a table near the back. They could still see most of the brightly lit parlor and the entrance but were mostly hidden from view. They placed their order with the young man named Benny who served as the waiter. Sonya mentioned that Benny was Louie's son. Family business, you know.

Derek and Sonya were laughing while eating their banana splits when the tinkling bell over the door made them look. When Sonya spotted the man and a woman who entered, she dropped her spoon with a *clank,* and froze. Her face turned pale, her jaws clenched, and her lips became a fine, tight line of hate. Derek noticed this change and asked her if she'd seen a monster. "Yeah. I did. That guy is named 'Rooster' Lock. He is a very bad memory from my past. Don't worry. He was never anything like a friend. Not now, but maybe someday when I know you better, I'll tell you about this asshole."

Derek leaned back having never seen this projection of intense anger in her before, nor heard Sonya swear. "He looks like bad news. His girlfriend looks like 20 miles of bad road too," he said.

They both laughed at that and it broke Sonya's grim mood somewhat. They returned to eating their treats and chatted about his next adventure trying to find a 4-year college to finish his degree. "I think I want to study criminal justice and maybe think about going to law school someday."

"Wow! That sounds like a lot of hard work. Why criminal justice?"

"Well, there are a lot of bad dudes even in our little city. The good people are constantly having to deal with muggers, thieves and such. I'd like to do my little bit to make this country a better place. I'm not sure what avenue in that subject I want to take, but I've been reading up on it. One of my friend's dad is a cop and I talked with him a lot last year."

His mother, he'd said, made him promise to graduate from college so he could at least be educated at something... or a lot of things. As with most mothers, Derek's mother (Maryanne) expected great things from her child. Derek did reasonably well in high school while excelling in basketball and baseball. Sonya remained quiet and a little subdued as she listened to his story and aspirations.

Then, out of nowhere: "Hey! Have you ever thrown a baseball? I'll bet with your strength you could really bring it."

"What do you mean 'bring it'?"

"Oh. Right. Throw hard."

"I've never tried throwing a ball. The only thing I've thrown around are other people." They laughed at that, and Derek said, "No. Baseballs are lighter and easier to throw than a body. And they bounce." More laughing.

"I'll have to show you how to do that someday. Have you ever played any other sports besides basketball?"

"Not really. Well, I worked at *kendo* for a while and got myself disqualified at a tournament. Does that count as a sport?"

"I don't know. What's *kendo*? Why did you get disqualified?"

"*Kendo* is Japanese sword-fighting. But instead of using real, steel swords, we use bamboo staffs. I hit somebody too hard and broke his bamboo sword. Knocked him down too."

Again, Derek looked hard at this very pretty young woman with the large, well-defined but definitely not ugly muscles that showed power. He saw a fierce countenance, yet feminine traits that made his heart beat quickly. Her hair was not long, but there was no doubting that, dress or no dress, she was all woman. She was simply a very special woman. Derek was eager to find out how special. It would take a little time, but his imaginings about Sonya Keller would fall well short of what she actually had in store for him... unknown to both of them.

Derek drove Sonya home and walked her up to her door. The expected awkward moment was dispelled when Sonya leaned in and gave Derek a brief peck on the lips. "Thanks for a wonderful evening. I enjoyed your company. It was good to get out. Will you call me again?"

Somewhat taken aback, Derek recovered from the kiss and said, "Of course I'll call you. Is tomorrow too soon? Maybe we can see how well you throw a baseball."

Sonya grinned and said, "Okay, I'll give it a try. Will you come get me, or do I have to drive to where we're going to play?"

"No worries. I'll come get you around eleven. Wear workout clothes and good, athletic shoes." With that cryptic remark, Derek smiled back and went down the steps toward his car.

"So, how was your first date?" Erica chimed as Sonya entered the room.

"It was fun. We had a very nice time. Derek is sweet, smart and seems to like me. The only thing that went wrong was that bastard 'Rooster' Lock came into the ice cream parlor while we were there. He didn't see us, but it felt like somebody poured cold water over me. Derek noticed it too and asked me what happened. I didn't tell him because I don't know him well enough. Maybe I'll never tell him. Otherwise, it was as good a first date as I guess I could expect. He's coming over tomorrow to teach me how to throw a baseball. Does this mean that my life is now in full bloom?" They both laughed at that and Erica got up and gave her tall daughter a big hug. She always enjoyed having Sonya squeeze her back so she could feel her strength.

Derek did in fact arrive at eleven sharp and Sonya was ready. She wore dark blue shorts revealing her firm, supple leg muscles, and a white tank top. She'd been wearing sports bras ever since she started needing them and wore her favorite one today. They were comfortable to work out in and flattened her chest so that her breasts, though moderate in size, wouldn't interfere with any of her movements. Derek had on long shorts and a T-shirt with the logo of Ball State University. Off they went to the ball field behind the high school.

They hopped the fence and walked out onto the infield. "Let's just play a little catch first. I brought an extra glove for you. I'm guessing you're right-handed. Okay. Good. I'm going to toss you the ball and you catch it in the pocket of the glove. Here's how you grip the ball when you reach in to take it out of your glove. Let me demonstrate the throwing motion."

This he did a few times and Sonya imitated him in synchrony with his motion. "Great. Okay. Let's play catch." He backed away about 30 feet and tossed the ball softly to Sonya. It hit the glove and bounced out and onto the ground. "You gotta squeeze it when it hits your glove." She tossed the ball back to Derek but threw it too hard and wide. He gave her a big grin. "Not bad for your first throw." After retrieving the ball, he tossed it to her again. This time, she grasped the ball as it hit the glove. She took the ball in her right, or throwing hand, and slowly went through the motion Derek had just taught her. This time the velocity was much more appropriate, and the direction was where Derek could catch it.

"Not as easy as you think, huh?"

"Don't worry. I can do this."

THEY SOFT-TOSSED FOR A FEW minutes with each of Sonya's return throws being more accurate. Derek corrected her motion a couple of times to smooth out the rhythm and define the release point. A few minutes more and she was throwing the ball back at about the same velocity as Derek was throwing to her. He started throwing it a little harder and as Sonya gained confidence in her eye-hand coordination, she was able to catch the ball and throw it back in some sort of good form.

"I'm going to now stand behind home plate and you're going to be the pitcher. I'll hold up my glove and you try to throw the ball into it. Start at about two-thirds of the way back to that white slab of rubber you see on that little hill. It's called the pitcher's mound." The look on Sonya's face was that she was starting to enter that realm of focus used in her martial arts workouts. Derek had never seen it before but noticed the non-verbal intensity building.

"Now take a stride toward me with your left foot and throw the ball to my glove. Put some real effort into your throw. Let's see what you have." Sonya took the stride and unleashed a missile that cleared Derek's head by 6 feet hitting the mesh backstop with a clinking sound. Derek looked back at her and slowly smiled. "Well, it's a little too soon to pretend to be Nolan Ryan."

"Who's that?"

"I'll tell you later." He picked up the ball and threw it back to her. "Step back to where you were. Let me show you how to turn your torso and release the ball in front where you see it going." Derek patiently led her through the pivot on the back foot, the opening of the hips and the stride all preceding the release of the ball. "Okay. Good. Let's do it for real."

Sonya's next throw was also wild, but Derek could catch it. "Release the ball in front where your eyes are looking." The next pitch was much better, almost a strike. Sonya kept concentrating and actually broke a good sweat. "Now, throw harder. Try to throw the ball through me."

Her next pitch hissed from her hand and smacked into Derek's glove sharply. "That's it. Great pitch. Bring it again." SMACK! As Sonya got the hang of pitching, Derek moved her back to the pitcher's "rubber" and showed her how her stride downhill would give her more leverage. It took six more pitches before Sonya felt comfortable enough to unleash her hardest throw yet. It stung Derek's hand with a loud popping of the glove. "I thought this might happen. You, my dear, are one strong athlete. How do you feel?"

"I feel great. Let's throw some more."

"Sure. Tell you what. Let's put you in the outfield. I'll throw a ball way up in the air and you run under it, catch it and throw it back to me as hard as you can. The trick is to hit me with the ball without me having to move much. Don't reach out for the ball until it's almost on you. If you reach out too soon, you'll slow down your run to the spot to catch it." He told her to run out into right field. Since he didn't bring a bat, he just heaved a high, arching throw out toward Sonya. She ran toward the ball but misjudged the trajectory and the ball landed behind her. "Throw it in."

Sonya's throw was on a line right into Derek's glove. *Oh my. She just uncorked a 200-foot bullet right into my glove. She may be the next* Natural. Next, he threw another high fly toward center field to make her run for it. Sonya took off, lined up the ball, caught it – though she flinched a little at being surprised by the velocity of the falling ball – stopped and threw toward Derek. Except Derek couldn't reach the throw. It was over his head, but as he turned, he saw the ball hit the screen behind him and stick in one of the openings. *Holy shit! I wonder if she can hit.*

Derek had to scale the backstop screen to un-wedge the ball out of it. After a few more throws from the outfield that stung his hand, he waved Sonya in and she trotted in toward Derek. "Let's see if you can hit a baseball with a bat. You told me about your *kendo* skills. I wonder if they will transfer to hitting a moving baseball."

"How are we going to do that?"

"There's a batting cage business near the college. Let's go over there and see if you can hit a few." They drove to the batting cage facility while Derek gave her a verbal primer about hitting a baseball.

Derek rented two bats and two helmets. He bought enough machine tokens for twenty-five swings each. They took the aluminum bats to the cage near the end of the line where Derek entered and gave Sonya more basic instruction about hitting with a bat in his hands. She gripped the bat and took a stance outside the cage as Derek showed her. He told her to stand directly behind him and swing when he swung. Derek set the ball speed of the automatic pitching machine to 80 miles per hour. For him, that was on the slow side, but he wanted to demonstrate more than achieve any real practice time. After lacing a few balls around the netted drop area, he motioned Sonya to step in. He put the machine on "pause", positioned her feet, set her stance and bat position. She took a few practice swings with just a little step with her left foot toward the pitching machine.

What happened next surprised Derek more than he thought he could be. After swinging and missing a few balls, she finally started making minimal contact, fouling off some more. Derek dialed the machine back to 75 miles per hour and the first ball Sonya saw at that speed she drilled to the back of the netted area. Then, she did the same to the next eight balls in a row, squaring up each and powering the balls out so that the nets were jumping.

"My hands are getting sore. The seams on the baseball made my fingers sore too. I think I've had enough baseball for one day. Buy me a cold soda?"

"Sure." They turned in the bats and helmets and walked into the tiny soda bar in the main building. Derek was somewhat stunned but was beginning to realize that Sonya Keller was an exceptional athlete and that nothing should surprise him.

"I gotta tell you, Sonya, I've never seen anyone pick up those skills like you did today. Baseball is not an easy game and hitting the ball like you did today takes most athletes years to develop. Are you sure you've never done this before?"

"YEAH. I'M SURE. YOU'RE A pretty good teacher, and after a little while it just felt natural to swing the bat that way. Throwing was a little harder, but then I found a rhythm for throwing. It just seemed easy once I got myself coordinated."

"Well, without letting your head get too big, I have to tell you that your basic skills are already ahead of most men I've played ball with. You probably can't catch the ball as well, but your hitting and throwing are almost there. Do you have any interest in playing baseball?"

"Not really. This was kind of fun, but I don't think I'm interested in a team sport. What else do you know how to teach me?" she said smiling broadly.

"Well, uh, how about handball?"

"What's that?"

"Two players are in a high-ceiling room and they play with a small, lively ball by hitting it with their hands against the walls while trying to get their opponent to miss it. Each player wears lightly padded gloves on each hand and hits the ball with the palms of their hands. At least, that's where you're supposed to hit the ball to get maximum control and power. Wanna give it a try sometime?"

"Sure. Do I get to run around this room all I want?"

"Oh sure. That's sort of the point. I should also point out that a player is only as good as his or her "off" hand. So, if you're right-handed, how adept you are with your left hand determines your ability to win games. Once an opponent finds your weakness, you're toast."

"Sounds like fun. Where can we play?"

"There are handball courts at the junior college. I'll see what I can do to get us a court when you're not working. My student ID still works, so it won't cost anything. But you have to go to the sporting goods store and get fitted for a pair of gloves. Also, buy a couple of handballs for practice on any wall you can find. Be sure to use your left hand more in practice until you feel it is as solid as your right. You'll see what I mean when you start practicing."

"You know so much about sports. I know nothing. My sheltered life kept me away from all these things. I'm enjoying being with you and look forward to learning more stuff."

"I'm glad. I enjoy being with you too. Besides your astonishing athletic skills and power, you just seem like a pleasant, nice person to be around. I like your sense of humor too."

Sonya laughed and then took on a serious demeanor. "I have my moments. I'm glad you think I'm nice. Sometimes I really don't know what I am. What I mean is that... like in that *kendo* match, I wanted to split that guy from top to bottom. Almost did it too. One day I'll tell you about what you might call my 'competitive spirit'. Do you have any suggestions for books that I should read? I was only home-schooled and read mostly textbook things. I don't know anything about politics, history or even what our Earth looks like. What do people write about? I see hundreds of books on shelves, but I wouldn't know what to pick first. My friend Kelsey told me about these sappy romance books she's read, but they don't appeal to me at all. I don't know what romance is. Is what we're doing part of romance?" she asked blushing a little.

"Maybe, Sonya. There is so much for you and I to learn about each other that I think if it comes on too fast, it will choke off whatever thing we have developing here. All we've done is see a movie, eat some ice cream and have you do to a baseball what only a few can. Listening to you open up is humbling and it sounds like you've needed to do that for some time. I'm listening. Also, don't be afraid to ask me anything. If I don't know the answer, I'll either tell you where to find it, or look for it myself. It's always better if YOU do the research. Otherwise, you could become lazy and too dependent on others."

"Well, I certainly don't want that. Thanks for your observations and thoughts. I've never really dealt with anybody in a kind of social situation before. Feedback in a social situation is brand new stuff to me. Or, as my *sensei* would say, 'I'm a grasshopper'."

THEY BOTH CHUCKLED AT THAT reference. "Look, Derek, I've enjoyed this time with you today too, but I would really like to get home and clean up. I'm all sweaty and I like to be clean. Will you take me home now?"

Derek drove her home. This time he kissed her sweetly and fully on the mouth before letting her get out of the car. She smiled back and asked him to call her when he could. Sonya then bounded up the stairs like a two-legged impala, looked back over her shoulder, waved and went inside. As she stripped off her sweaty clothes, she felt an inner tingling not felt before and wondered if she was falling in love with Derek Murphy. Oh, she knew she loved her mother, Kelsey, Ned and Evelyn, but this seemed different. *In the showers, NOW!*

Chapter 10

"WHAT DO I DO NOW?"

"SO, HOW DID THE BASEBALL day go with your new, hunky boyfriend?" asked Kelsey over the phone.

"It went okay, I guess. He taught me how to throw, catch and hit a baseball. Derek's a pretty good teacher and seems sweet. What's up?"

"Just checking to see how your 'coming out' is going. I've even had a couple dates at school with a very smart math whiz. He's cute too. Maybe we should double-date sometime. My guy's name is Andy Schwartz. He's got a head full of this kinky dirty blond hair, wears glasses, but is kinda handsome and hunky too. He plays tennis and is trying to teach me that game. It's *HARD!*"

"I know what you mean. The first time I tried to throw a baseball, I threw it almost over the backstop at a 100 miles an hour." They both laughed. "Why do guys try to teach us new sports?" Sonya asked.

"Well, I can see Derek trying to teach you stuff. He saw how you moved on the basketball court and in the studio. Andy saw me playing basketball at the gym. See, I met him in chemistry class as lab partners. He thinks I'm pretty hot too." More laughter.

"Now, Derek wants to teach me handball. I told him that team sports didn't do much for me and the baseball and bat made my hands hurt. So, now he wants to get me alone in a big room to bash a small, black ball around. Weird."

After a little more banter, Sonya asked Kelsey, her one and only confidant, about her feelings for Derek. "I think I'm really liking this guy. He even kissed me a couple of times. I know, I know. Big deal, right? Well, for me it IS a big deal having never been kissed before. Look, I've seen enough movies to know what is supposed to happen next, but I'm really afraid to let my emotions go toward the 'L' word."

"The 'L' word?"

"Yes. LOVE, dummy."

"Oh! THAT 'L' word. So, are you getting heart palpitations and getting a little warm in those certain areas?" Kelsey teased.

"Yes, smart ass. And I don't know what to do about it. I'm thinking about Derek all the damned time. What do I do now?"

"Well, if you trust him, just go with it. Is it the past stuff that has you freaked?"

"Yes. It's taken me a couple years just not to flinch away from a man when I meet one. This is a whole new ballgame, and I am scared shitless."

"I don't blame you, but only the baddest of the bad are like those guys who assaulted you when you were just sixteen or seventeen. Most guys don't know what to do with women like us. Smart, strong, beautiful women intimidate most men. Both of us are all of those things, so it's the guys who should be scared shitless, not us." They laughed heartily at that commentary.

"So," Kelsey continued, "just let the dates go as they will. When he tries to put his hands on your tits, you will have a decision to make. If you like him enough and he has a good touch, let him do it. The rest of that progression is up to you but be sure you have protection available if it gets to that point."

"Oh, god! I can't even think about that. I've been feeling that I need to tell Derek about my past experiences, so he'll know why I am so nervous about being on a date. When we were having ice cream and that bastard Rooster came in, I must have turned different colors, because Derek picked right up on it. I told him I'd tell him about it later. Does it seem right to you that I should tell him about the rapes before we go too far?"

"YES. HE HAS TO KNOW sooner or later if it's going anywhere, and if you kind of freak out in the middle of something without him knowing why, it might blow the whole thing to pieces. So, yeah, tell him, but only when the time is right. Trust your intuition here. You'll know when that time is right. Because I love you like my sister, I can only tell you to be your own best counsel and respect Derek's person and how he treats you. If there is a major change in his treatment of you and your time together, drop him right away."

"Thanks, Kelsey. I need to hear all that. Fragments of those kinds of thoughts have been bouncing around in my head for a while, but I don't know how they fit anywhere. You help me organize coherent thoughts from the fragments. What would I do without you?"

"I hate to think about where you would be if you hadn't escaped to our house that horrible night. I'm thrilled to have you as a sister, and don't want anything but happiness and good things for you. You'll always have me as your friend, confidant and sounding board. Any time, of any day. You need me, I'm there for you."

"Thank you, even though I've always felt that. I hope you feel the same things coming from me. Kicking those punks' asses was my way of showing that I love you too."

"Well, don't kick my ass while you're all so full of love." More gales of laughter.

"Okay. Gotta go. Mom will be home soon, and I've got to get dinner started. See you soon."

"Yup. See you soon. Have a nice evening. Are you gonna talk to your mom about this, uh, subject?"

"Yes. She needs to know. We share so much, don't we?"

"True that. Take care. Love ya."

"Love you too."

Sonya busied herself in the kitchen getting dinner ready. Erica walked through the door at her usual time, smiled and greeted her beautiful daughter with a brief hug. "Let me change out of my work clothes. Fix me a martini, will you?"

Sonya fixed the martini just the way her mother liked it and added the single green olive. Perfect. Erica limited herself to one drink only at any time, having seen first-hand what overdoing drinking alcohol could do to a person's mind and behavior.

When Erica emerged, Sonya handed her the cocktail and sat down at the table. "Mom. I gotta ask you what you think I should do. It's about Derek."

"Uh, oh."

"No, it's nothing bad. I'm just not sure what to do or how to go about conducting my side of a budding relationship with a boy. I think Derek really likes me, and he seems to be all good guy. I haven't seen any of the danger signals that scare both of us. Thing is, I really like being around him even though it hasn't been very long. How will I know what to do? What if things get physical? I mean, I've read all the books and seen how these things go in the movies, but now I have my own script to read."

"Well, baby, all I can say is keep working it out. Trust your instincts. God knows, we have enough of the negative shit to draw on in our experience. I'm glad you mentioned danger signals. We both know what they are. Hell, I'm still so twitchy that I can't hold a 10-minute conversation with an unmarried guy. I don't know if I'll EVER let myself go and allow myself to fall in love again. But your just twenty, I'm forty. You have everything in front of you, and, God knows, you are very strong and capable of defending yourself in any situation. If you're asking for my advice, I'm going to sound like an old song and just say listen to your heart. It'll tell you what to do."

"Thanks, Mom. Just talking about it helps. Kelsey and I talked earlier, and she said about the same thing. I guess this is part of the learning I need to have confidence in myself."

They exchanged hugs and Sonya went back to fixing dinner. Tonight, it was going to be her special meatball recipe in some hearty red sauce to put over linguini. A nice, cold salad and a glass of dark, red wine would top off the menu for tonight. Erica didn't mind that Sonya drank a little wine, because they both operated on the knowledge of what *out-of-control* drinking looked like. That wasn't them. It could never be them.

Sonya turned in earlier than usual saying she had some work to do at the studio when she got up. Ned had been increasing her workload giving her more responsibility and duties with the business and, aside from teaching a few classes and staying in shape with her own workouts, she was learning how to run a business and make a profit doing it. She saw less and less of Ned, but knew he was just a phone call away should anything serious arise. Sonya took in the increasing responsibilities with relish and worked harder every day. She even suggested repainting parts of the studio as some of the paint was peeling and fading.

Upon reflection during quiet time, Sonya felt that the arc and momentum of her life were definitely taking a turn for the better. Maybe this is what *Sensei* Nelson meant when he told her about a balanced life and how that balance between all aspects of one's life made one much more capable of handling every aspect, decision and outreach with the best that person could offer each area. It used to sound like just abstractions to Sonya, but now, with Derek working his way into her life, that operating philosophy made more sense each day.

With each passing day, maturity became the lesson, and the question, "What do I do now?" became less a question of confusion and more one of "Let's see how good an outcome I can make of this situation."

Chapter 11

WHEN YOU GOTTA STEP UP

SONYA WENT TO BED EARLY one evening but didn't go right to sleep. She sat up in bed still fully dressed contemplating all that was swirling in her mind. The very existence of Derek Murphy pushed her mind to a completely different place from anything she'd ever known. It was not even a path that was parallel to any other. Her deeply embedded drive to rid society of those creatures who harm innocent and good people for money was the path she had put ruts into by running along it for so long. Now, this *boy* was giving her emotional agenda a twist, a spin into something good and lovely and caring. This was, she realized, the first time that these paths had even been seen in her mental picture frame at the same time. She felt that it was going to take some time to figure all this out. Maybe the separate paths were there for her convenience, meaning she could take one or the other – or both – at her leisure. Maybe they were going to intersect. Maybe they were going to both be part of her life as separate paths suggesting that she might have to live two lives, each one involving separate compartments of intensity, emotion and significant energy. She realized that her hatred, anger and sense of right was a white-hot bed of coals, but Derek's presence was a cooling presence to those particular embers. Seeing that bastard Rooster blew pure oxygen across those coals, and she almost let Derek see that. On the other path, she felt the emerging glow and warmth of emotional coals growing for Derek and their time together.

I'm only twenty. I have a lot to learn and do. Maybe Derek is the fuel for that separate and different bed of coals. Can both beds of coals burn hot? Will one or both of them burn me? Will either or both of them finally burn out in time? Time will tell, but won't I be necessarily in charge of how long those coals burn hotly? How will I know when they cool?

AFTER MORE PONDERING ABOUT HOW she would deal with her more basic and primitive emotions and instincts, her eyes grew gritty and her eyelids heavy. She undressed, turned off the lights and fell into a deep sleep, a sleep given to the righteous.

The next morning, Sonya's buzzing phone woke her. "Hullo," was her still half-asleep greeting.

"Good morning, sleepy head. It's Derek. Sorry to wake you, but I wanted to catch you before you made other plans."

The sound of Derek's distinctive, baritone voice snapped her out of her slumber. "That's okay. What's up?"

"I just got handed two tickets to a White Sox game against Cleveland for tomorrow night. These teams are fighting for first place. Wanna go?"

"Uh. I guess so. What time? I have to close the studio at five. Is this a baseball game?"

"Yes. Don't you know anything?" he chided.

"I guess not. Should I bring a jacket or something?"

"Yeah. It'll probably get chilly after the sun goes down. Sometimes the wind off the lake can be cool, even in late August."

"Where are we going? Chicago?"

"Yep. Pick you up at five at the studio. I'll even spring for hot dogs at the park."

After hanging up, Sonya rolled over and tried to imagine what going to a baseball game would be like. She'd never even seen one played on television. She was going to sound really stupid. *But Derek seems to be patient and a good teacher. I just hope I ask good questions.*

She went through her usual morning routine of showering, dressing and eating a light breakfast. Her first class was at nine o'clock today. She went to the studio and powered through her day of teaching classes, had lunch with Ned, did her own physical workout and did the necessary book work. She told Ned about how things were developing with Derek and confided that she was scared to commit even though she liked being with him a lot. She mentioned that he asked her to a White Sox game tomorrow night. That "confession" was met with a broad smile, a big hug and some kind words meant to instill confidence in her judgement of character. "You've experienced the worst in humanity first-hand, but you gotta accept that the vast majority are good folks. Maybe this Derek is as good and decent as I am. Besides, if he's taking you to a ball game, he's gotta be a good guy. And you know that if anyone should treat you, my second daughter, with anything but decency, I will descend upon them from a very high place." They both laughed, hugged again. Ned returned to his office to make some calls.

The next day sort of flew by for Sonya. She only had two classes, so she was able to shower after the two o'clock and get ready to go to the game with Derek. At 4:45 she closed the books and made sure the alarms were set and the office lights were off. She locked up at five sharp and there was Derek waiting out front. She hopped into the car and gave Derek a big smile. He leaned over and kissed her sweetly sending a mild shiver through her body. Off they drove into Chicago traffic along the Dan Ryan Expressway where they exited to get to Guaranteed Rate Field on West 35th St. "Who would name their stadium 'Guaranteed Rate?'" she asked.

"People with a lot of money. See, the baseball team sells naming rights to increase revenue so they can pay their players millions of dollars. I think the minimum wage in major league baseball is close to $500,000 per year – give or take. The big money boys are making upwards of $25 million per year. There seems to be no ceiling. Are you sure you don't wanna be a ballplayer?" They laughed.

"Really? $25 million? And they get to wear those dorky looking uniforms too? What more could anyone ask for?" They shared the laugh while Derek was parking near the very back rows of the parking lot down by 37th and S. Princeton.

"Wow! The lots are filling up quickly," he said. "It might be a sellout tonight. Big game." The glow of the stadium lights beckoned to the people streaming down the walkways to the big ballpark.

"This neighborhood doesn't look too hot over there," Sonya mentioned.

"No. Those are some of the low-rent projects. Lots of gang and drug activity around here. It can be pretty scary sometimes."

They walked the few hundred meters to the entrance gate at the ballpark and were told that their gate was around the other side. They were plenty early and the teams were just ending batting practice. Sonya watched with interest as the ground's crews spruced up the field while Derek went out to the concession stand to get them a hot dog and soda. She was struck by how *green* the grass was under the LED stadium lights. Their seats were in the upper deck just above the visiting team dugout, but only three rows from the railing. The entire panorama was before her and she started getting excited for the game to begin. Derek returned and they wolfed down their hot dogs while the PA announcer gave lineups over the sound system and told everyone to stay off the field. *Why would anyone who wasn't playing want to go onto the field?*

Some local police unit honor guard walked onto the field and a slim, black woman sang the national anthem. Everyone stood with their hands over their hearts as the singer's soulful rendition filled the park with her great, resonant voice. Everyone cheered and the home team White Sox trotted out to their positions in their startlingly white uniforms. Sonya started asking questions about the names of the positions the players were in. She recognized the pitcher and the catcher, but the rest were mysteries that Derek was happy to explain. The first pitch from the White Sox pitcher was loudly called "strike one!" and the crowd cheered. Derek quickly explained the concepts of balls and strikes and outs. Strikes were good for the team in the field, after all, baseball was the only game where the defense had the ball. Hits and runs were good for the team at bat. And the game had no time clock. In fact, if the score was tied after nine innings, the teams played *extra* innings. How cool was that? His instructions of the basics were laced with little quips and humor that reflected more than a century of baseball tradition and rules. Sonya smiled happily as she started to grasp the totality of the game.

During the first three innings, Sonya peppered Derek with all sorts of questions some of which he couldn't imagine anyone asking. But he did answer them, and Sonya seemed to become more interested. It was not a dull game. Right from the beginning, hitters had the game going their way and the Chicago clean-up hitter even hit a long home run. Sonya was the last to stand up and cheer, because she, at first, didn't see the point. Once she got into the game, however, she was cheering and yelling along with everyone else. Derek took great joy seeing her emote out of the corner of his eye. He'd not seen her excited like this before and, as with everything else about her, it captured more of his heart. *I'm doomed and all-in to fall in love with this wonderful woman.*

The game was indeed a sell-out and by the seventh innings it was Chicago 9 and Cleveland 8. There were some breathtaking fielding plays by the home team that also brought the crowd out of their seats to applaud. The Indians rallied in the top of the ninth to go ahead 10-9, but Chicago's pinch hitter in the bottom of the ninth hit a two-out, two-strike home run with two runners on base to win it in walk-off fashion, 12 - 10. The crowd went wild and Sonya appreciated the excitement of it all, jumping up and down like everyone else.

The crowd was slow to calm down and even slower to leave their seats and head home. Derek and Sonya dodged the crowd for a while, until Sonya spotted a rest room and ran inside. Derek did the same and they met several minutes later to continue their exit back to their car. By the time they got all the way back to the general area where their car was parked, most of the other cars had departed and they were almost alone as they walked. It was kind of dark in this back corner of the lot and they could just make out the silhouette of Derek's car.

Just as they approached the car, a man in a hooded sweatshirt jumped out from behind it and pointed a gun at Derek and Sonya. Sonya saw that it was a Smith and Wesson .38 snub-nosed, double-action revolver. The mugger's hand shook a little as he stuttered out his command.

"Gimme all your money or I'll shoot you!"

The mugger took two steps closer threatening with the pistol. Derek started reaching for his wallet and Sonya saw the mugger's head turn slightly in that direction. Ned had taught her how to defeat a revolver of this type a dozen times in a dozen different ways. In a flash, her left hand grasped the pistol in a vice-like grip preventing the cylinders from turning. With a double-action revolver, squeezing the trigger set off a two-step action: as the hammer came back, the cylinders turned so that a new chamber was present when the hammer fell. By jamming the cylinders with her grip, the gun was unable to fire.

As she gripped the pistol, she spun under the mugger's arm twisting it and his wrist so hard that Sonya could feel the tendons and ligaments tearing as she relieved him of the gun. In one motion, she spun around and, using the butt of the gun still in her hand, cracked the mugger in the back of his head dropping him to his knees. This move was followed by a swift and accurate kick to the mugger's solar plexus, winding him completely. As he struggled to rise, Sonya, with the speed of a striking cobra, drove the heel of her right hand under his chin causing teeth to break and his head to snap back hard, leading the rest of his body to the ground. He appeared to be out cold.

She looked around and saw that there were no spectators. Without another thought, she opened the pistol and extracted the bullets. She then walked over to the nearest street, Princeton, and found a storm sewer drain into which she threw the bullets and the gun. "Let's go. We've had enough excitement for tonight, haven't we?"

Derek stood there with his mouth hanging open. He nodded and unlocked the car. There was still some adrenaline running through them both, but Derek managed to get the key into the ignition and start the car. Sonya was still breathing a little heavily but looked composed.

"Baby, I had no idea you could do what you just did."

"Well, sweetheart, I teach this stuff every day. If he'd had an automatic pistol, it probably would have been a lot more exciting for everyone. That kid will remember this night for a long time, or until his next drug dose. Hey! You really know how to show a girl a good time!"

That broke the tension and they both bent over laughing. Derek responded with something very lame that sounded like, "You're the best, most protective date I've ever had." They both howled with laughter as the adrenaline cooked off. Derek found his way back to the freeway and drove them both back to Gastonburg. When Derek stopped next to the studio, he didn't have to lean over, because Sonya was in his arms before the engine stopped running. They kissed long and hard letting the emotions of the evening carry them along.

When they leaned back and caught their breaths, they both smiled broadly. Sonya pushed away and said, "I gotta go. I've had enough excitement for the night. I'm still trying to find my bearings in all this. I enjoyed the baseball game too. Thanks for being such a great teacher."

"And thank YOU for saving our asses tonight. He could have killed us both."

"Naw. Had it all the way," she joked. "When the whistle blows, you gotta step up." With that, she was out of the car and gone to her own.

Derek sat there for a few more minutes watching Sonya drive away, waving to him out the window. *My god! What kind of woman have I fallen for? Brains, beauty, guts and POWER. What the hell do I do now?*

Chapter 12

TRANSITIONS

SONYA AND DEREK CONTINUED DATING, one of which included her introduction to handball. Typical of her physical prowess and rapid skill acquisition, she hit the ball so hard, that she broke two of them. The force of her blows also hurt the palms of her hands. She did enjoy the physical exertion and sense of athleticism necessary to play the game, though. This game helped her see the value of cross-training between different physical activities. She and Derek also became more physically affectionate as Sonya learned what tenderness was, something she'd never experienced before. Her emotional trust in Derek grew as did her comfort being near him.

So, naturally, just as their mutual desire to spend as much time together as possible, as bad timing would have it, Derek had to leave for Ball State in Muncie, 200 miles to the southeast. His newly received basketball scholarship required him to live in campus housing. It was a Sunday, and Derek had to report to the players' dormitory by five o'clock. "Well, while I'm at BSU, maybe you should sign up for some classes and GJC," he suggested.

"That's a good idea. Ned has allowed me a pretty flexible schedule, so I can probably squeeze in a class or two." For the first time, Sonya felt the tug of sadness at someone leaving her. They agreed to call or write or e-mail every chance they had. Derek suggested that she learn how to run *Skype* on her computer so they could actually see each other while talking.

"I'd better not see any women's underwear in the background, buddy. I might discover what jealousy means."

After a brief chuckle, Derek took her by the shoulders, looked straight into her eyes and said, "You're the most amazing woman I've ever met. I want our relationship to continue and grow. When I commit to someone, I stay committed until they give me a good reason to break that bond. I think we have a lot to teach each other and I truly enjoy being around you. It seems that every day brings out something new in your personality. I look forward to the day when you trust me enough to tell me of your past... which I suspect is, uh, difficult."

"That's nice to hear. I've never felt this close to a guy, ever. Not even my father. I'll tell you more about that later. I'm feeling more relaxed and trusting around you all the time. And yes, my past is very difficult. You may not like what you hear, but if we're going anywhere, you're gonna have to know. Right now, though, let me kiss you goodbye, pat you on your head and wish you safe travels. Muncie isn't that far away, but it'll seem like a 1000 miles to me."

They kissed and embraced. Sonya did indeed pat him on his head while smiling away the tears in her eyes. As Derek drove away, Sonya turned and let her real, pent-up emotions go. She sobbed openly and produced rivers of tears. But these weren't the emotions of hate and revenge. They were the emotions of loss, disappointment and maybe even the beginnings of true love. She'd been having more moments like this where her conflicts surfaced and battled each other. Still, the personal scars and the abhorrent, skin-crawling reactions she had for the drug culture, its dealers and the victims drove her to seek some sort of purpose. She was now able to maim, even kill those who she felt offended and destroyed the decency of men and women, people like Kelsey and her own mother.

How dare they be allowed to go unpunished!

First thing Monday morning, Sonya drove over to the junior college with her transcripts and high school graduation certificate. She enrolled right away and signed up for a class in post-Civil War history. From her conversations with Ned, Evelyn and Kelsey, she wanted to know more about how those stories of terror and brutality had their roots so far back in our nation's past. Ned and Evelyn's family came from the era of lynching, church burning and horrifying, race-based brutality that decried anything resembling a civilized culture and society. How was it possible that so much hate and rage could be directed at people the attackers didn't know, but just for the color of their skin? She felt she needed to know how this puzzle worked.

Her class would start in one week. She bought the textbook and some note-taking supplies, returning home in time for lunch. Then, it was off to the *do-jo* for her afternoon classes.

She felt energized at work this day and worked her students extra hard so that everyone was sweating and panting. "Good! I'm glad you're tired and sweaty. Life is not just an elevator ride to the top floor. It's not a taxi ride downtown. We have to work our bodies so they can serve us in times of need. If you're in a time of stress, you want to be able to endure your attacker or attackers' assaults and make them pay. Fatigue and weakness makes us all cowards. Go rest, eat a good dinner and I'll see you all on Wednesday."

The somewhat disbelieving class of eight women and two men looked at Sonya in a new light. She'd never talked to them like this before. They knew she was correct, of course, but they didn't expect to be talked to like she was a football coach. As Sonya grew into her new position of instructor, her classes and mini lectures became both more challenging and oriented to the real world.

She worked her second and third classes just as hard while getting more physically involved in the lessons than normal. She hadn't been working out as much lately and felt herself slipping. *That can't happen. I've worked too hard to get to this point. I've got to stay sharp and in shape.* After that personal pep talk, she locked up and ran home, leaving her car in the parking lot. She would run back the next day for work. She saw Ned that next day and showed him her GJC class schedule; nine o'clock to ten thirty, Monday, Wednesday and Friday for the next 6 weeks. "No problem, Sonya. I'll be interested to hear what your teacher has to say."

The Gastonburg Junior College campus covered fifteen acres of trees and nicely landscaped commons areas. The building architecture was modern colonial with lots of red brick and bright white trim. Brick paths crossed the green lawns all across the campus creating arrows of direction between the classroom buildings. There was even a student center where students could go for a lunch or just a soft drink. There were quiet study rooms in the basement.

The history class met in a small amphitheater-style room located in a building named Florence Hall. Apparently, somebody named Florence donated lots of money to the school and got this lovely, quaint, red-brick building named after him... or her. Sonya didn't know which.

About fifty students showed up and almost filled the room. The seats all had those fold-up note tables that never seemed to be big enough to write on. A nice-looking black man sat down next to Sonya and smiled. She smiled back. "Name's Butch Reynolds. How ya doin'?"

"Sonya Keller. So far, so good... but it's early. This is my first class here at GJC. You?"

"Nah. I've been coming since I graduated high school. This is my last year here; gonna get my JC credential. Gonna go be a cop."

"Really? Wow! What makes you want to be a policeman?"

"Just tired of seein' my homies and 'hood being eaten up by gangs, drugs and shootings. I wanna do something about it. What are you doin' here?"

"My boyfriend (*Oh, my god. I said it*) is off to Ball State to play basketball, and suggested I start taking classes. I'm just trying to find out what I like before deciding what I want to do in school... if anything."

"That's cool. What's your boyfriend goin' to study?"

"He's not sure, maybe coaching or teaching. Maybe criminal justice. He really is good at sports. He even taught me how to throw and hit a baseball and play handball. You ever play that game?"

"Yeah. I love hitting the ball around the room. We should play sometime."

"Okay. I'm not very good yet. I've only played a couple times."

"That's okay. I'll go easy on you," he said, laughing. His *Sonya Surprise* was just around the corner.

Just then, the presumed instructor came in from a side door at the front of the classroom. Everyone quieted down and the man spoke. "Good morning. My name is Devon Hullaby. I'm here to help you learn about our American history after the Civil War ended in 1865. If you're in the wrong class, be on your way. Otherwise, listen up." Hullaby was a tall, thin, medium-colored black man with a decent Afro hairstyle. He wore "granny" glasses, a white shirt, necktie and dark tan, corduroy trousers. His voice was rich and resonant. He proceeded to call the role from his roster annotating absences. "Anybody here who I didn't call?" One hand went up. "See me after class and we'll get you signed in.

"I'm not a 'doctor' – yet. I have a Masters of Arts degree from Northwestern and am working on my Ph.D. So, 'Devon' or Mr. Hullaby or Mr. 'H' will work. Let's try to respect each other while we get to know one another. When you have a question, raise your hand and tell me your name. If I ask one of you a question, correct me if I've mis-pronounced your name. I don't keep a seating chart, but if you miss class, I'll know, because your assignments won't be handed in. Yes, you will hand in a little something every day. Why? That's to get you involved in the material and *keep* you involved. This is not a 'memorize dates, people and events' class. Oh, you'll learn these things, but my intent is for you to learn them in the context of the times, the events of those times, the actors, their actions and the consequences of those actions. That way you'll have several pegs on which to hang your memory hats. Everyone good with that?"

There was a murmuring of agreement and Mr. Hullaby continued with his opening-day speech. It culminated with him writing their assignment on the board: *read Chapters one and two. Answer the questions at the end of each Chapter, then, write a short essay about what mattered going forward from those particular times.* Hullaby expected them to do twice as many hours of out-of-class work as the 90 minutes spent in it. He promised there would be discussion periods every day, so that being prepared would avoid embarrassing "I don't know" moments.

"You gotta be ready to know history, because today is tomorrow's history. It's a moving target that never stops," he concluded.

After class ended and everyone was filing out, Butch asked Sonya for coffee, and they went to the cafeteria at the student center. They chatted about various things including more details about Butch's environment. He told her about how his mother stood up to his drunken, smack-addled father when he was only five, and literally threw him out of the apartment in which they lived. "She was a powerful woman, my mom." He went on to expand on his life story, one that included all the gang activity and how they tried to recruit him as a runner for their drugs when he was just seven years old. They often went hungry until his mom could get paid work doing laundry or house cleaning for the white families on the other side of town. Somehow, working the odd jobs until she literally dropped dead from exhaustion when Butch was twelve, she managed to save a little money so Butch could pay the rent until he found work somewhere. She'd always insisted that he go to school every day even though they lived in a run-down building with fights almost every day.

There was one teacher, however, who spotted the promise in Butch Reynolds. His name was Howard Smith, and he hired Butch to do yard work and help him build his garage. Mr. Smith was a white man who insisted on teaching in Butch's school precisely because they needed his knowledge and teaching skills so desperately. He was not a coach and taught science and government to juniors and seniors. Through his connection with Howard Smith and his dedicated wife, Gloria, Butch learned some carpentry skills, some automobile repair and maintenance skills as well as experiencing a no-strings-attached love from a white man and woman. When the Smiths found out about Butch having no parents and how he shuffled between abandoned buildings, they went to work building a room in that same garage for Butch to stay, sleep and study. They felt that it was the least they could do for a young man with such promise and good heart. Still, the black kids in the school rode Butch mercilessly about that relationship with Mr. Smith causing Butch to defend them with words and fists. The drug culture continued to infest the school and the old neighborhood from which he came. Somehow, he made it through without being expelled, graduated and was now in college. The Smiths still employed him and kept his room orderly for him when he came home.

Sonya assured him that skin color had nothing to do with the pervasiveness of drugs. The drugs went wherever there was money, hopelessness, pain, poverty and the lack of parenting. She told him she'd seen it all, while not revealing any specific details of her former home life. What began as a serious conversation changed into a cheerful chat about sports until they both ended up staring into their cups. In an attempt to break the mood, Sonya asked, "Butch, do you have a girlfriend?"

"Yes. She's studying pre-law at Ball State too. I met her in high school. She had Mr. Smith for science too, so we sort of worked together on projects and stuff. She wants to be a public defender. I told her that if we were gonna get married that one of us will have to earn some good salary money. PDs don't make shit." They both nodded.

"Do you have a picture?"

"Yeah." He dug the picture out of his wallet and showed Sonya a pretty, round face with dancing curls and flashing dark eyes.

"She's beautiful. What's her name?"

"Olivia Gordon."

Before he could say more, another young male student pulled up a chair and invited himself into their conversation. "Hi."

The intruder had a name. Butch introduced him as Delvin Barkley. Delvin Barkley was light-skinned with rusty, curly hair down to his shoulders. He had the facial features of an African-American, but also had green eyes and a splash of freckles across his nose and cheekbones. "I see how you look at me, girl. My mother is white, and my father is almost white. So, now you can stop gawkin' at me like I'm from Mars, or somethin'."

"I'm not staring at you because of your appearance. I'm wondering why you felt it was okay just to drop in and interrupt our conversation without saying excuse me, or something like that."

"Well, *excuse me,* Missy. I had no idea that you were so fucking important and polite," he said, putting on a "step-n-fetchit" stage accent. Sonya grabbed her backpack and got up to leave.

"Wait, Sonya. This fool didn't mean nothin'. He's just rude to everybody."

"Yeah. Well, I don't care much about being stereotyped just as much as he doesn't."

Delvin chimed in, "I'm truly sorry. I just saw my man Butch googly-eying some pretty white girl while his main lady is away."

"Well, as a matter of fact, uh, Delvin, Butch was just showing me her picture. Is your girlfriend as smart and good-looking as his?"

This put a cloud over Delvin's face, and he got up, snorted and stormed off. Butch said, "I like it that you didn't take any of his shit, Sonya. He tries to bully everyone he sees. No self-respecting girl will even look at him, green eyes or no green eyes. Besides, I think he has a drug problem too. Don't know for sure, but he seems especially weird sometimes. Look, I gotta go to my next class. See you on Wednesday. Study hard." Butch flashed her his best smile and went in the opposite direction Sonya was heading, back toward her car.

On the way past one of the classroom buildings, Delvin popped out and stood in her pathway. "You know, I didn't care much for your mouth, bitch. Who the hell do you think you are? You just some pink-assed bitch with a big..."

Before Delvin could utter another word, Sonya's right fist was exiting from the indentation it made in his solar plexus. He folded up like wet paper. She bent over his gasping form, grabbed him by his hair, and said right into his face, "The last motherfucker who called me a bitch is still healing from broken bones. For the sake of your health, I strongly recommend that you leave me the fuck alone. Can you understand all those syllables strung together? Can you?"

Delvin nodded dumbly and started to regain his breathing. "Why did you hit me so hard? I didn't mean nothin'."

"Look, pal, jumping in a stranger's face with your bullshit is a sure way to get yourself some hospital time, especially when you don't know what that stranger brings to the table. No hard feelings, Delvin. Just learn to have better manners and treat women with respect. You just never know when one of them might actually find a way to like you."

Sonya stalked off, and Delvin, still clutching his gut, looked after her as if he'd seen a ghost.

Well, that was an interesting first day at college.

Chapter 13

MISSION CREEP

THE WEDNESDAY HISTORY CLASS BEGAN with Mr. Hullaby stating that in order to understand what happened after the Civil War, one must understand the history of slavery in this country and how it formed the economic and social stratification culture that we still endure. "The Civil War didn't end with the signing of the peace treaties. With Lincoln gone, his plans and views for an orderly and compassionate reconstruction went out the window. The South was, of course, decimated, and the opportunists from the North flooded that defeated country to exploit all its weaknesses and shattered infrastructure for the sake of easy profits. The resentment from the white people left in the South was certainly understandable as they also watched their former slaves take over farms and plantations and even voting. This situation created a short-lived, but bizarre situation where black men were actually elected to government and even Congress. With most of the white men killed and unable to rebuild their homes, towns and culture, and women not having the vote, only the black males were left to govern. Pretty ironic, don't you think?

"I'm not going to get into the origins of slavery other than to say that indentured servitude or slavery has been around since the invention of economics and agriculture, for about 10,000 years – maybe longer.

Christopher Columbus brought slaves to the "New World" to work the new sugar cane industry. It just mushroomed from there. Okay. When the southern whites finally got back on their feet, they pushed back hard on reconstruction. Their seething resentment took the form, of course, of rejecting the emancipation of black people and actually organizing resistance movements based on racism. The KKK, for example, was started by a former Confederate General, Nathan Bedford Forrest. Since southern white culture never saw black people as anywhere near equal to themselves, no matter what their social ladder status might be, they took their rage, frustration, feelings of oppression and defeat out on white northerners and black people. In other words, the post-Civil War southern culture was based on hate and resentment from the end of the war and into even today. In the broader view of history, who can blame them? There were no healing missionaries between North and South. In fact, northern politicians tried to exact retributions for war damages from the eleven Confederate states even though there was NO economy whatsoever and no help in re-establishing one.

"So, your assignment for Friday is to research and find anecdotal evidence for what I mentioned in today's lecture. Write a couple pages about your discovery and be sure to cite them properly in a bibliography. Have a good day."

Butch and Sonya just looked at each other with amazement. At almost the same time, they said, "I had no idea..." They laughed a bit and went off to have their coffee and chat.

"I hear you had a run-in with my boy Delvin after our coffee on Monday."

"Yeah. He confronted me and started calling me names while getting in my face. Sorry. I just don't take that shit from anybody."

"Well, he's had that coming for a long time. He's a good kid on the inside, but I think he's been bumpin' up next to some druggies and I think he's tryin' to cop the bad-ass attitude of that bunch."

"Yeah, well, he's not the only one who has experienced drug-altered behavior." She briefly told Butch about how her mother and herself were abused by her father and his drugged-out pals. She didn't include the most sordid details, but Butch was rendered silent.

Finally, "Holy shit. Who'd want to mess with a beautiful and obviously strong woman like you?"

"I wasn't always this big and strong. I started working out after the worst part of those events. I moved in with my girlfriend's parents and learned martial arts and physical training. I have a couple of belts in various disciplines including *kendo*."

"WHAT'S *KENDO?*"

"Japanese sword fighting. They use bamboo swords instead of the real thing. It's pretty ancient and goes back to the 18th century, or earlier *Samurai* culture. I got pretty good at it but busted a sword over the head of some former champion. I got kicked out of a tournament for doing that."

They both laughed, but then Butch looked at Sonya in a whole new light. "So, let's play some handball tomorrow morning. Let's see what you got."

"Great. I could use some cross-training work."

Sonya went to the school library early on Friday to do her research for her class, next day. Around nine-thirty on this cool, early autumn day, she went to the gym and changed into her handball court clothes. She discovered at the appointment desk that court 3 was reserved for Reynolds. Butch hadn't arrived yet, so she went into the room to practice by herself. After about 5 minutes of warm up and left-hand drills, Butch walked in smiling and started warming up himself. Butch noticed Sonya's body parts exposed by her shorts and tank top. *Damn! This girl has some serious physique!*

They tossed to see who served first and Butch won. He ran up three straight points before Sonya could stop his serve with a high lob that almost stuck to the back wall. Her first serve shot past Butch like he never saw it.

Her next serve was a killer that caught the side wall and the floor almost simultaneously just past the foul line and squirted at a right angle from the side wall. Her third serve shot right back at Butch's belly. He jumped to get a glove on it, but it deflected. Three – three.

"For somebody who hasn't played much, you sure as hell know what you're doing."

"I have a good teacher. Derek is very good and kicks my ass all over the place."

"Well, from the looks of you, you can do some ass-kicking too."

"That's how I got my two black belts." They both laughed.

Sonya's quickness around the room stretched Butch's physical ability to its fullest extent. Eventually, though, his experience found Sonya's weak spot, picking lob shots off the back corners, and he prevailed.

"I've gotta get cleaned up and go to work. Thanks for the game, Butch. I enjoyed the workout."

"Me too. With a little more experience and practice, you'll be able to hold your own with anybody, man or woman. How did you get so strong and quick?"

"It's weird. It just sort of was there all along but didn't come out until I started training. Oh, and I'm a pretty good pistol and rifle shot too. My teacher was a Navy SEAL and taught me all sorts of stuff. Want to meet him?"

"I just might. I have to get in shape for the police academy physical and tests after the new year."

On the way to her car, Sonya passed one of the poster kiosks. A stapled poster caught her eye.

Party at Lenny's
Saturday night. Live band. Free drinks and munchies.
Bring a friend or come on your own.
873 Bannock; 8 o'clock.

Sonya wrote down the address. This getting out more started seeming more and more like a good idea. *I wonder what a house party is like? I guess I'll find out.*

This was the busiest Sonya had been in her memory. Between her workouts that kept her body rock hard and her martial arts skills sharp, her self-defense classes and now schoolwork, she seemed to have little time for herself. Erica asked her if she had too many things going on more than once. "I can handle it so far, Mom. If I get too stressed or start missing work or school, I'll cut something out."

Saturday night was cool even for early October. Sonya wore tight-fitting yoga pants and a long, loose sweater that came down almost to her knees. Under her sweater she wore a flexible Lycra top that came up to just below her chin. She thought that would be sufficient for the evening. Not wanting to be the first one there, Sonya arrived a little before nine o'clock. There were about fifteen people there and the band in the back yard was already rocking. A girl from her history class recognized her and invited her over to the bottles of beer and soda in a large tub of ice. "You're that tall girl in my history class. How are you liking Mr. Hullaby?"

"He's fine and seems to be bubbling over with information. I'm really having to work hard at taking all his notes."

"Oh, I'm Marjory Ellis. What's your name?"

"Sonya Keller. Nice to meet you."

"Same here. Well, help yourself to whatever you want and maybe some guy will try to pick you up," Marjory said laughing.

"This is the first house party I've been to, so I don't know what to expect."

"Well, the band is pretty good, and I'll bet they'd love to have you in their audience."

"Good idea." With that, Marjory evaporated into a group of people. Sonya did, in fact, wiggle her way through a group of animated talkers and out to the back patio where the band was going strong.

Sonya pulled a cola out of the ice tub and found a chair. After one of the songs, a guy came over to her and said hello. He asked her to dance. "Sure. Are you a good teacher? I don't know how to dance." Then she stood up. The young man was only about 5 feet 6 inches and his eyes and head kept rising upward as Sonya rose from her chair.

"Uh. I guess so. You're tall! Well, just kind of let your body move to the beat of the music. Focus on the drums and bass. You can move your feet almost any way you want. Ah. Here's a good one to dance to. My name's Art."

"Sonya. Like this?"

"That's it. Just let your hips and shoulders get in time with the bass line. Good. You're a natural."

After the first dance, the band changed tempo and a slow dance started that everyone seemed to know the words to. "Do you dance slow?" Art asked.

"I don't know. Let's find out."

Art showed Sonya how to hold his hand and where to put her other arm. When he put his arm around Sonya, he blinked and looked up into those killer blue eyes. "Wow! You've got muscles. And they're hard. Are you a professional athlete, or something?"

"Sort of. What do you do?"

"I try to study economics, but right now I'm trying to learn how to not be intimidated by a tall, beautiful woman."

Sonya laughed. "And who would that be?" With that, she tightened her grip around Art's waist and lifted him off the ground as she spun in a circle. After she set him back down, they both laughed.

"Don't be intimidated, Art. I'm a gentle soul until somebody messes with me. Thanks for accusing me of being beautiful. I haven't been out much, so I have no idea how the world sees me. See, I teach self-defense classes and my students see me as teacher or *sensei*. And we're all sweaty and panting from the workouts, so beauty isn't one of the items of interest."

"So, are you an expert at *karate?*"

"Yeah. I have two black belts in that and other disciplines. So, don't worry. I'll protect you from any bad guys who attack you." Her beaming smile and twinkling eyes disarmed Art to the point of rendering him silent.

"Thanks for the dances, Art. Let me retrieve my soda."

"Sure. Okay. I've never been slung around a dance floor before, so that's a new one for me. Nice meeting you, Sonya. Maybe another dance later?"

"Maybe. Bye, Art."

Sonya watched Art disappear into the growing crowd, but as she walked over to the ice tub for a fresh cola, she looked up and saw two men that chilled her blood and bristled her neck hairs. They were "Demon" Smith and Jimmy Raymond. She'd been seeing those faces in her nightmares for years. *What the hell are they doing here?*

Immediately lapsing into her stealth training, she looked for nooks and crannies where she could see or follow them without them noticing her. Her sweater was navy blue, so she didn't stand out. *Sensei* Nelson in Chicago had taught her well. It didn't take long for her to see what they were up to. They were clearly older than just about everybody at this party. Their body language spoke: prowling... like predators. Sure enough, she saw "Demon" pull something out of his jacket pocket and hand it to a sloppily dressed boy. The boy then passed some bills back to "Demon". She looked across the room and saw Jimmy doing the same with a couple of girls.

Sonya wondered if they remembered her. A plan was forming, and she needed to know if she had automatic cover. She walked right up to "Demon" and smiled right into his face. "You want some candy, little girl? Well, you're obviously not little, but would you like something anyway?"

"No thanks." She smiled and walked away. *He doesn't remember me. Good.* Next, she found her way over to where Jimmy was hustling drugs and repeated her spontaneous greeting. Nothing. He didn't recognize her either. Sonya then retreated into the dark recesses of the house. Art found her and asked her to dance. She politely refused and said she was getting ready to leave, thanking him.

After about a half-hour, the two drug dealers walked to the front door and left. Sonya counted to ten, then followed them out, sticking to the shadows. She saw them walking toward a blue panel van. She noted the license number and took out the pen from her small fanny pack and wrote it on her hand. She watched the van pull out and drive slowly away, turning left at the next intersection. The plan was forming more quickly now.

ON MONDAY, WHEN SONYA SAW Butch for class, she asked him if he knew somebody who could run a license plate for her. "Yeah. My mom's uncle is a long-time desk sergeant downtown. But he'll want to know why I want this. It's not legal to give this information out without a warrant or something. Invasion of privacy, you know. Fourth Amendment stuff. You'll have to find out yourself somehow."

The history class this day was more than Sonya bargained for as Mr. Hullaby introduced the class to the enormous struggles the poor and the people of color had to endure across the country even as it expanded across the plains to the west coast. The plains Indians were attacked and slaughtered by U.S. Government soldiers, cheated and exploited by whiskey and disease and packed away on reservations of the poorest land. Hunting cultures were forced to become agrarian, and agrarian cultures were herded onto land where little grew... or could grow. While this was going on, Sonya learned that black people were streaming north to find work and to avoid the lynchings in the South. As the southern whites regained their hold on their communities and economy, they excluded blacks wherever they could and in the most brutal ways. There was no such thing as welfare in the 19th century, and many families, both white and black, starved. Lincoln's dream of reconciliation was never taken seriously by the white-dominated Federal Government. Worse, the black people moving north took jobs for half the wages that white workers demanded for the same skill sets. Instead of white worker resentment being directed at the capitalists and businessmen who hired the cheaper labor, it was directed at the black workers. Thus, casual racism in the north was replaced with a more virulent strain. Segregation and overt racism became an overall national phenomenon rather than just a regional one.

Sonya had never been exposed to this level of understanding about race. Even with her father being such a perfect shit, he never brought the subject up. Then, of course, the drugs destroyed any remnants of rational – or even irrational – thought or conversation. Meeting Kelsey and her family seemed as natural to Sonya as putting on her shoes; Sonya didn't even think of race until Ned and Evelyn mentioned their experiences growing up in the South. Derek's mother was white, and his father black. So what? He seemed to be a good guy, so why should skin color be a limiting factor in who one befriended? Learning the history of hate, prejudice and bigotry helped her answer those nagging questions. *I guess if that stuff is pounded into your head and is seen everywhere you go, it becomes part of you. But the inherent wrongness of it... It makes no sense. But not all white people or southern white people are prejudiced, are they? How did they get away from that swirling vortex of bigotry? Did they just decide to not hate? Did they actually sit down with themselves, their church leaders or their friends to help them make the mental leap away from it? It just seems natural to me to accept good people no matter their skin color. We have students come to the studio who are of just about every race one could imagine. There seems to be good camaraderie among us. Maybe the bigotry and the prejudice gets too much attention. Then, maybe there shouldn't be any of it at all. Well, the hate, prejudice and bigotry are the problems of others, not me. My anger and feelings are directed at those who abuse others with drugs, gangs, violence and thieving. Those things kill innocent people and destroy communities.*

Mr. Hullaby was introducing history as a thought process as much as just a recounting of dates, places and events. Understanding the context of major events gave much more meaning to how we are the way we are as a nation and a people. Why, for example, was our lust for land such a big deal that we literally stole it from the people who had lived here for 10,000 years before Europeans decided they wanted it? Why didn't our European ancestors ask for permission to share the vast reaches of our continent? Sure, the Spanish were seeking gold to pay for their endless wars, just like the Romans did. And, like the Romans, the Spanish empire foundered, though the nation itself didn't collapse. The Vikings were itinerant warriors and conquering adventurers. It was in their culture to invade and plunder. They didn't last long in North America or Greenland, though. They couldn't defeat the aboriginal Americans in Canada. Then, it was the turn of the English. Except that after the Pilgrims and the Huguenots escaped the vagaries of the European churches and sailed to the Americas uninvited, they decided to stay and expand their hold here.

Hullaby tried very hard to connect all the dots preceding the Civil War without bogging the class down in the masses of details from all of Western Civilization's history. The highlights he put forth were dramatic enough. The details also gave the students a kind of scaffold upon which to base their essays and research yielded from their homework. "Oh, and by the way, history, like science, is a never-ending process. Today is tomorrow's history," he often said.

One day, after class, Sonya caught Mr. Hullaby as he departed. "I'd like to talk to you about the history of the drug culture and why poor people seem to be more affected by it."

"Sure. What are you doing now? I've got an hour or so before a faculty meeting. Let's go to my office."

Sonya didn't have to say much before Hullaby started in on the chain of events and how humans have always seemed to want something to alter their minds. "It's this thing about having a very large brain that actually perceives abstractions. Pleasure has a whole different meaning for humans than it does any other animal, I guess. No other animal seeks non-nutritional intake for the sake of pure pleasure. Okay. Maybe cats and catnip, but it's not an addictive thing for cats, is it? They don't know it's catnip. They just like getting buzzed... I guess." They both laughed at that.

"But more to your point, Ms. Keller, poor people live in a lot of misery and pain, mostly from frustration, hopelessness and envy. Poor people don't know they're poor until they see wealthy people sportin' things they wish they could have. Big cars and fine clothes become status symbols in the poor areas, even though those people are still poor. That exposure to symbols of wealth changes everything. Doing drugs in the 'hood is a two-edged thing. First, drugs are the escape mechanism for those who feel they have nothing else. It's different for poor men than it is for poor women. Poor men do the drugs as part of the bonding experience with each other. Poor women do drugs to kill the pain of being treated badly by men, the pain of being hungry and the misery of watching their children starve and wallow in squalor; they are helpless to change that and feel crushed by the hopelessness. Drugs cover that pain. Then, it's all they live for. This completes the circle of poverty.

"These are broad statements, but the urban black culture in northern cities stems from what I lectured about the other day when discussing the post-war migrations from the South. The drug industry is easy money for everyone involved. Like any other industry, it knows its customer base. Okay? The black customer is usually different in motive than the white customer, but once those customers are hooked, it doesn't matter what the skin color, or socioeconomic status. All junkies look and act the same and for the same reason.

"The rich, white people who do the expensive drugs like powder cocaine and heroin do it because they can, and they can get away with it. Why do you think the prisons are upside down with racial convictions for drugs? The white people can pay for the lawyers, the hopelessly poor black druggies can't. Add to that, most judges in drug courts are white. You get the picture.

"So, we have, in this country and many others, the perfect market and customer bases for making tons of money for everybody up and down the chain of drug dealing. The demand drives the supply, and demand is almost more than the supply chains can provide for. We're talking about a nearly $6 billion per year industry. So, take that little five-dollar bag of rock and do the math. Yes, Ms. Keller, our children and our nation are being slowly poisoned to death and nobody seems to be able to do what's right to actually treat the cause of the drug addiction and pervasiveness. And that cause is mostly poverty. Employ people with dignified work, and the pain mostly goes away. Show them they have purpose and meaning through productive work, and the chin comes up off the chest and the person stands a lot taller. It's hard to bend over to snort a line when you're standing so tall with pride. Instead, our governments and police, just knock heads and throw people in jail. Guess what happens when they get out? Yeah. That's right. They go back to the 'hood and start dealing and using all over again. Why? Because that's all there is for them. No good jobs with dignity attached. No good schools where they can learn a trade. No good places to live where the rats and the roaches don't compete with the humans for dinner. Sorry for the rant."

"Don't be sorry. It's exactly what I wanted and needed to hear. So, what IS the answer? How do we treat the cause instead of the symptom?"

"I'd start with upgrading the inner-city schools on a massive scale. Included in this overhaul would be an emphasis on vocational training. In parallel to that, I'd institute a kind of modern-day CCC where we take the idle kids and adults, train 'em to do carpentry, electrical, plumbing and such.

Pay 'em a decent wage. If they don't come to class and work, they don't get paid. There are all kinds of unemployed journeymen who would train these kids. Government pays for the tools, the supplies and materials as well as the salaries. What do they do? They re-build the shit holes in their own neighborhoods. All those abandoned homes, buildings and apartments get gutted and re-done with energy saving and alternative energy technology built in. That's what the kids and adults would be taught to do. Studies show that for every dollar paid to working folks, ten dollars of economy is generated. When these kids are getting paid, they're going to BUY those expensive sneakers instead of shooting someone and taking them off their feet. That kind of thing. Yeah. I know. I'm a flaming idealist, but by providing real hope for personal growth at the community level, the crime plummets and the gangsters become secondary artifacts of times gone by. You can look it up. In fact, I hope you will look it up."

"I've heard of the CCC, but has this ever been tried in big cities?"

"Yes. After WW II, General George C. Marshall gave President Truman his plan to re-build the destroyed cities in Europe and Japan. It was called the Marshall Plan and only cost the United States about ten billion dollars. That's a lot of money, but that investment generated two to three orders of magnitude in economic returns, and by showing up the Soviet Union in the process, it helped undermine that un-democratic form of government. It's hard to put a monetary value on the amount of goodwill that was also generated. The eventual collapse of the Soviet Union is directly linked to the Marshall Plan. All the other stuff about the Cold War is mostly bullshit and distractions from what was really happening in the West."

"Wow! I've got a lot to learn. Thank you SO much for this lesson. Someday I'll tell you about how drugs impacted my family and my life. I think you'll be interested in my plans. I feel I'm on kind of a mission, and now the mission just moved up a couple clicks. It's kinda creeping along, but it is creeping toward something that will matter a lot... I hope."

"Well, that's intriguing. Are you going to sell tickets to your mission? How long will mission creep last before we see some results?"

"I'm not sure, but I'll tell you in code when it does. You deserve to know."

"Now, I'm REALLY intrigued. I hope you have a good plan and that it is a safe one."

"No worries. I can take care of myself. I teach self-defense classes. Nobody will want to mess with me," she said laughing.

"Okay. See you in a couple days. I look forward to reading your essays. Gotta go."

Chapter 14

TRACKING AND TRAPPING

SINCE BUTCH COULDN'T HELP HER find out who owned that blue van, Sonya kept notes of the parties being advertised on campus. She drove to the addresses and waited to see if the blue van showed up. Finally, at one of the parties, she saw the blue van parked near a house. She didn't have to wait long before Demon and Jimmy emerged laughing. She followed the van at a safe distance for several blocks until it turned onto Western Way. It drove up the driveway of 1313. The name on the mailbox said "Beddell".

So, Sonya thought, *this guy Beddell is now running drugs at college parties. Of course. That's where the money was, and the inhibitions weren't.* She wondered if Beddell also ran the street "vendor" business in the neighborhoods. The name Beddell nagged at her memory. She felt certain that she'd heard it before.

The car her mom had purchased for her last year was as nondescript as she could find. Nobody looked at a dark gray Toyota something. It had a roomy trunk for all her stuff, ran quietly and got good gas mileage. At night with the lights off, it was virtually invisible. Perfect. She would begin the stakeout tomorrow.

1313 Western Way was a modest, off-white, one-story bungalow with a driveway that curved all the way to the back of the property. An orange muscle car of some sort was parked at the curb in front. Sonya drove to the next block and parked facing away from the suspect house. She adjusted her mirrors so she could see the comings and goings. She'd had the good sense to bring a lunch and a couple of water bottles. It was time to wait... and take notes if anything happened.

About an hour and a half later, a very large, muscular young man emerged from the front door and got into the muscle car – how appropriate. She had taken down that license number on her first pass. Finally, Smith and Raymond exited, got into the van and started to drive away. Sonya started her car and turned around to follow them. Sure enough, the men drove to the campus and started scanning the message boards. Occasionally, they wrote something down. When they left, Sonya visited the same boards and found party notices. She wrote those down too. She planned to be a special kind of party girl in the coming nights.

That Friday night, Sonya dressed in her "combat" gear underneath a long, loose sweater and went to the first party on the list. There were two parties scheduled this night. She hoped she would catch her prey at the earliest one that was closest to Western Way. She sat in a corner, virtually invisible to anyone coming or going through the doors. As luck would have it, her two targets entered together at just after nine. She slipped out of the front door and found their blue van parked a block away. She took out the potato she'd brought along and stuffed it up the tailpipe of their van far enough where they couldn't see it. She waited.

The two druggies exited the house counting money and walked toward their van. It started up and they pulled out of their parking spot, but when they were just halfway out, the engine quit. They ground and ground, but it wouldn't fire. The lads got out cursing and lifted the small hood of the engine compartment. "Having some trouble, boys?" Sonya asked as she pulled up her mask.

"Naw. Wadda ya want? Know anything about cars?"

"Not much, but I know a lot about other things including drug dealers selling poison to kids."

Just as "Demon" reached toward his belt, Sonya kicked his left knee hard, tearing several ligaments. She whirled and hit Jimmy with a straight punch to his jaw with her gloved right fist. "Demon" kept reaching for his weapon and Sonya stomped his hand, kicked him in the face, then knee-dropped onto his sternum. The gun came out and she kicked it across the street. Meanwhile, Jimmy was recovering consciousness and trying to get up. Sonya's next kick caught him from behind right where his testicles were, and thus displaced them. She walked over to where the pistol lay, ejected the magazine and ratcheted the round out of the chamber. As she had done before in Chicago, she dumped the gun and the magazine in a storm sewer opening.

"Here, let me give you a little something to remember this evening." With that, she pulled out her short sword and sliced one of their Achilles tendons just above their attachments to their heels with swift, single strokes. It wouldn't start hurting until they tried to walk, because the calf muscles would roll up like a window shade. "That should keep you away from the party scene for a while." She then took all the money from their pockets and wallets. While walking back to her car, she called the police on a burner phone to come clean up the streets. She tossed the phone into the sewer too. She could now hear the distant screams of the two dealers. The drugs they had left on their persons as well as in the van would be enough for the police to get a good, solid collar, especially for convicted felons.

It was a good thing that Sonya masked her face, because across the street, an aged woman had pulled back her curtain when she heard the boys cursing their vehicle. When the police questioned her, she said she saw a large, darkly clad figure take the two boys down. She remembered seeing a flash of metal in the streetlights but couldn't see the face of the attacker. After the attacker started to leave, she turned away to call the police and didn't see any other cars pull away. Sonya had parked around the corner from the party house where prying eyes wouldn't get too close. She also placed opaque cloths over the license plates and removed them before driving away. Nobody would know who she was, or even if she was a male or female. Perfect.

Sonya drove back to 1313 Western Way and resumed her stakeout position. Around midnight, Mr. Muscle and his orange car came screeching up the driveway. Beddell, with his long ponytail bobbing in the breeze, met him on the stoop and they entered into a very animated conversation complete with waving arms and door slamming. Seeing Beddell's face in the porch light reminded her of who he was. He was her father's first drug dealer. Mr. Muscle ran back to his car and screeched away with Sonya at a safe tailing distance with lights on dim. The orange beast finally pulled up in front of a run-down apartment. Sonya parked where she could see where he went. He ran up to one of the upper units and started pounding on the door. No answer. Mr. Muscle looked around and then kicked the door. He flew inside. Lights came on. Sonya had the window rolled down and could hear a great thrashing sound as if the apartment was being tossed by an angry bull. After a few minutes of this, Mr. Muscle came out onto the balcony and pulled out his phone. Sonya could plainly hear, "Oh SHIT!" The police must have called Beddell about his van allegedly being stolen by drug dealers.

Mr. Muscle pounded down the stairs and ran to his car and zoomed away. With more than a little curiosity, Sonya went up to the destroyed apartment looking for some information she could use to further Beddell's misery. What she did find among the wrecked apartment was a logbook with names and delivery dates with a code in another column that could be for the types of drugs dispensed. In the right-hand column were dollar amounts and dates. This could be valuable. She slipped out and back to her car before she heard any sirens. She guessed that loud noises in the middle of the night were not unusual to this complex.

She returned once again to 1313 Western Way to see the next bit of activity unfold. The muscle car had returned, and all seemed quiet. Lights blazed inside the Beddell house. After waiting for an—hour, or so, an unmarked police car pulled into Beddell's driveway and two plainclothes policemen got out. It was time to go. Sonya drove slowly home and called it a night. She did what she set out to do but knew that getting greedy would be dangerous and foolish. *Let 'em sweat for a while. Let them try to figure out who is doing what to whom.* Meanwhile she had this logbook to decipher. Maybe she could find some of the street drug networking to disrupt by reading it more closely.

Chapter 15

TAKIN' IT TO THE STREETS

"WHAT'S NEW WITH YOUR, UH, 'investigation'?" Butch asked.

"Oh, just trying to find out who is who. I suppose it's time to tell you my story. I haven't even told my boyfriend this story, but I trust you. You still wanna be a cop, right?"

"Now, more than ever. My sister got mugged over the weekend and had all the stuff in her purse stolen by some punk."

"After class, I'll tell you a story that will, uh, straighten your hair." They both laughed and agreed to have coffee after class.

Mr. Hullaby gave an impassioned lecture about the horrors and failures of reconstruction and the evolution of Jim Crow laws in the South. There were a lot of moans and groans from the mixed-race student body when he delved into the methods of lynching for the most minor and frivolous acts of black men and even some women. Even if a white man, for example, accused a black male of any age of trying to flirt or even make eye contact with a white female, without trial, that black man was dragged to a lynching tree, hanged, castrated and sometimes burned even after he was dead. Most of the class felt the chill of savage racism as they left class and there wasn't the usual banter and chatter as students filed out.

At the coffee shop, Sonya and Butch began their conversation with a summary of their emotions about today's lecture. "Well, on that note," Sonya said, "let me tell you about the rape of my mother and myself by my father's drug merchant and user pals."

"What? You and your mother? And your father was involved? Holy shit, Sonya!"

"I was just seventeen and weak as a kitten. My mother escaped to a battered women's shelter after I got raped and I ran to my girlfriend's house. That's where I met her parents and learned martial arts. My friend Kelsey's father was a Navy SEAL and runs a martial arts studio. When my mother recovered and my father got out of jail, he came after my mother again and beat her blue for selling the house and filing for divorce. Can you imagine that? When that happened, 2 years after the rapes, I had just tested for my first black belt and was able to lift some serious weight in the gym. I think I told you what I can do now, but back then it was almost as much. I'm stronger, faster and can jump higher than most men my size or even bigger. Anyway, my father was set up and had the living shit beat out of him with several bones broken. He ended up in the hospital for months. He was a convicted felon carrying a gun, so the judge threw the book at him and put him away for a long time. There was no evidence and no witnesses. The attacker is still unknown.

"But his three pals served their drug sentences and are now out roaming around, back to selling drugs... or at least two of them WERE out selling drugs. Remember that van I told you about? Turns out they are using that van as transport to kids' parties around town where they sell their drugs. I watched them do it when I went to one of those parties.

"So, I'm still traumatized by my experiences with drug dealing bastards. When I see and hear about what goes on, I see all sorts of colors and other bad stuff. My girlfriend even got attacked by three guys wanting her money to buy drugs. They beat her pretty badly. I found out who they are."

"Holy shit, Sonya. It's good you're not confessing anything to me about what you did. I'd have a lot of trouble with that."

"Right, and I will not tell you any more. I am who I am and am not the least bit remorseful about what happens to those slime balls running the drug networks. When you get out of the academy, we'll talk more. We're partners now. I've got your back."

"Okay. And I've got yours. Nobody should have to deal with what you did... from their own father for Christ's sake! You go do what you gotta do. Just be careful and be safe. Always leave yourself an escape route."

"I'm good. I'm highly motivated and very, very good at planning."

"Cool. You're one hell of a woman, Sonya. Does Derek have ANY idea what he has in you?"

"Not yet, but he soon will." They both laughed at that and went their separate ways for the day.

Sonya spent some time at her desk in the studio trying to figure out the logbook she acquired the other night. Some line items showed large numbers in the coded column, with large dollar amounts after them. There were six names that kept repeating and were associated with those large numbers. The only conclusion she could make was that these were street dealers, while the rest were smaller, individual transactions. Most of those didn't even have names attached.

There is an area of Gastonburg known as *drug alley*. There, cars troll slowly along until the drivers spot someone lurking in an alley or a doorway. It is the nighttime events that give this area of dark streets in the poorest part of town that name. Virtually every citizen paying the least bit of attention knew of its existence but were not involved with trying to clean up that neighborhood. It was, after all, the place where "those people" lived. The embedded racism there, as it is in almost every town and city in the United States, prevented real intervention and policing. "It's always been this way," is the cop-out phrase used when people are too dismissive of "the other" to really care. The irony, though, is that most of the revenue for those drug dealers and distributors is generated from the white middle classes and upper classes who drive their Benzes and Beamers through there to "score" some drugs. After all, what's a hot party with hot babes without a few lines of *blow* or a pipe full of *meth*? Yes, even in small towns like Gastonburg there are such parties made up of such people. After all, where should those hotshot money-makers go or what should they do once they descend from their glass and steel offices of commerce and industry in nearby Chicago? They must relieve the stress of those high-pressure business deals and horrible commutes to their sacred bedroom communities, after all. The stay-at-home spouses also need some manufactured chemical outlets after long days of cooking, cleaning and wiping runny noses, don't they? Soap operas and midday vodka will only get one so far, won't they?

Sonya Keller had decided some time ago that she wasn't going to sit idly by, wring her hands, nor cast aspersions on "those people". "Those people" were the products of American society just as she felt she was. She was as much a victim of the drug culture as anyone else who indulged, profited and died from its influence on the people close to her and not-so-close to her. She knew she had a personal score to settle, but it had now, in her mind, expanded to feeling she was doing something worthwhile. It wasn't right by any standard that scum bags like Raymond (just call me Ray) Beddell should get rich at the expense of others who became his addicted clients. Worse, Beddell's suppliers and higher-level traffic organizers were getting even richer. She had read the articles of drug kingpin take-downs in Mexico and in Texas where entire attached garages and inner rooms were stacked, floor to ceiling, with pallets of cash, American currency. Where did that money go? Who got to spend it? On what did they spend it?

The demise of Pablo Escobar in Columbia gave some insight. He funded, through his drug trades, the salvation of the dirt poor. Of course, once they accepted his largesse, they were beholden and became part of his network.

He used the money to also pay off the police, both local and governmental. Honest police and judges and officials were assassinated if they tried to interfere and actually apply the laws of their land.

So, in a cynical extension of this situation, the United States' illicit drug demand was funding a good portion of the economies of third-world countries. Coca farms and ranches became going concerns and the farmers, for the first time in their lives, lived in some other shelter than those with dirt floors. This begged the question, "What would happen to them if Americans (and others) stopped demanding cocaine? What would those poor farmers do? How would they live?"

Sonya understood, but couldn't fathom doing anything about that bigger picture. She knew she was just one person with a self-imposed mission. She would take action that she could control in her own community where her loved ones and friends lived. She was constantly reminded of the violence and death-dealing that the local drug trade brought about. She was going to be the biggest pain in their asses that they'd ever known. Clearly, the police were inadequate or not interested enough to pinch off the source of the drug culture in Gastonburg. Fueled by her embedded rage from her past, she set out to visit the streets and do what she could to make her town cleaner and the citizens feeling safer. She didn't wear a cape, but she felt she was something of a crusader.

In her evenings after she closed the studio, she began patrolling and surveilling *drug alley,* changing her route and her observation points regularly. Her gray car was so innocuous as to be noticed by nobody. Good. During her tours and stakeouts she charted the activity of each dealer she located. The ledger she obtained from "Demon's" apartment indicated six street dealer activities. One evening, she saw the orange muscle car drive down one of the streets, park by an alleyway between two dilapidated apartments and wait. Out from one of the apartment buildings came a tall, slim, dark man in a hooded sweatshirt. He went to the passenger side of the car and bent over to look inside. A large hand emerged from the window holding a wrapped package about the size of a loaf of bread. The hooded guy took it, turned around and went back inside. Sonya decided she would come back after her mother went to bed. She didn't want Erica to start worrying about her missions or her activities.

She parked in a different location around eleven that night. There was very little foot traffic and even fewer cars. She waited. About eleven fifteen, a dark blue Mazda sports car slowed down and stopped between the two apartments. Out from the alley came the same hooded guy and made the obvious transaction with the Mazda. Sonya had changed into her "work clothes" that included a small, compact fanny pack that held her special equipment for the night's activities. She crept silently into the shadows of the alley. Her camouflaged action suit was dark gray mixed with panels of lighter and darker areas separated by vertical lines. This, she had learned, was what urban camouflage was meant to do: blend in, look like a wall, no human body outlines.

She came to the corner of the apartment building and let herself ooze around the corner into the alley. She practiced her footfall techniques to avoid making any noise of movement. She held still for several minutes to allow her night vision to adjust. Soon, she made out images and outlines of the dealer, his chair and table and the usual dumpsters and broken furniture of the alley. It was a dead-end alley as the buildings turned and met about 50 meters from the sidewalk. She waited. The dealer seemed to be nodding off. Finally, he lit a cigarette and she could see his facial features by the lighter's dim flame.

She didn't know the face, but he was quite young looking. There was a scraggly mustache and wispy goatee, but no other distinguishing features. The hoodie was frayed around the edges and there was no drawstring around the hood. The kid sat and smoked.

Finally, another car pulled up at the mouth of the alley, this time a gray

Mercedes. The kid got up and slowly walked out to the car. Sonya positioned herself behind his chair making sure she wasn't silhouetted against any backdrop. The kid sauntered back snapping the crisp bills and stuffing them into his pouch. He sat down not seeing Sonya at all. With a quick movement of both her gloved hands, she slammed her open palms against his ears. The pain must have been excruciating. The kid screamed and leaped from his chair. Sonya kicked him squarely in the groin sending him to the ground groaning in pain. While he was incapacitated, she used her great strength to jerk his arms away from his balls and secure them behind his back with cable-tie handcuffs. She then did the same with his ankles. Finally, she connected his wrists and ankles with another cable tie such that he was cinched up firmly and barely able to move. She then picked him up by his belt and carried him to the street, plopping him down under the streetlamp. She wanted him to be found. A potential customer would see this and bolt for safety. A local neighbor might call the cops, but she hoped that Mr. Muscle would come by to check on his street guy. *This should have some impact on the customer base for a while,* she thought ruefully.

As she drove home, the adrenaline and tension from all the controlled and careful movements finally unloaded and she started trembling. She was immensely thirsty and drank three glasses of ice water when she got to the apartment. The clothes came off and into the washing machine. She showered and let the hot water on her nakedness wash away the night's work. When the adrenaline finally burned off, she felt enormously tired and fell into bed and a deep sleep.

When Sonya awoke the next day, it was already late morning. She drank coffee, ate some breakfast and pulled out her brand-new assault rifle from under the bed. It was the Navy variant of the M4A1 made by Colt that was more compact and easier to handle. She'd hidden it after buying it last month so her mother wouldn't worry. The gun store owner also sold her his special, privately loaded ammunition that featured smokeless powder. She'd been practicing at the range Ned had previously taken her to and had learned the discipline and elements that all good snipers learned and possessed. It was getting time to use those skills for a more noble purpose... or so she surmised it to be.

She read from one of Ned's Navy SEAL books how to fashion her own flash and sound suppressor. The commercially sold ones were quite expensive. The rifle took most of her savings. It involved packing a plastic water bottle with steel mesh dish scrubbers surrounding a central tube of fine wire screen between the muzzle of the rifle and the outside. She took along some duct tape to secure the "silencer" to the muzzle. When she got to the range, she went to the firing position at the far end. She took three shots to warm up and made a nice grouping. Then, she taped on the suppressor. She fired again and found that there was no hindrance or loss of accuracy with the suppressor in place. She hit the bullseye three straight shots. The sound, instead of the sharp crack from the 5.56 mm NATO rounds, was muted to that resembling dropping a melon onto a hard floor. *Good.*

Her night-time surveillance yielded another dealer outlet very similar to the one she exploited two nights ago. But this location had some nearby abandoned buildings with flat rooftops. Sonya picked one of the abandoned ones, a four-story brick urban blight candidate and found her way up to the roof. Along the way, she placed luminous strips of tape so she could find her way up and back without using a flashlight. She would peel them off on her way out after her next mission. She scouted the roof and found a nearly perfect shooter's position that faced the alley mouth just a little more than 100 meters away.

The next night was cool and cloudy, so there wouldn't be any moonlight shadows. After her mother went to bed, Sonya dressed in her "gray man" gear and slipped the rifle into its carrying bag. She parked two blocks away from her sniper position building and moved from shadow to shadow to its opening where she slithered through the doorway. In the dim light, she took the rifle from the bag and taped on the noise suppressor. She carefully followed the trail of tape up to the roof. By carefully creeping along near the middle of the rooftop, she avoided any silhouetting until she was proximal to her post. Cradling the rifle in her arms, she low-crawled over to the edge and peered over it to view the alley mouth and the street below.

There was a single, dim streetlight half a block away, but the 4.5-14 x 50 mm rifle scope, with its excellent lens coatings, would allow enough light in for easy viewing and aiming. She waited. Finally, along came an older, gray Chevy with a broken taillight. It stopped by the alley opening. Another kid in a dark, hooded sweatshirt emerged and went over to the driver's window. A transaction occurred quickly, and a handshake of sorts was shared. At that moment, Sonya squeezed the trigger on her Colt and felt the slight kick in her shoulder. Through the scope, she saw the hoody kid spin and hit the ground clutching his wrist and screaming. The driver stuck his head out to see what had happened and Sonya saw that it was none other than her father. She fired a round into his left rear tire. Tempting though it was, she held further fire and called the police on a burner phone to report shots fired and the license number of Crummy's car. As a twice-convicted felon, to be caught in this situation would be more hurtful to him than just conveniently ending his suffering. His next visit to prison would be much longer as a repeat offender and parole jumper. She smiled to herself at the prospect of Crummy's old friends waiting for him when he came back inside.

On her way back to the descending stairs, she dumped the burner phone down an air vent. Peeling off the luminous tape as she went, Sonya got back to her car before the sirens got too close. She was home in minutes and felt satisfied about eliminating or greatly interrupting another death dealer in her community. No remorse. Another bad guy down. And Crummy will once again visit his new, and most intimate friends in jail.

Chapter 16

UNRAVELING THE NETWORK

THE PHONE BUZZED NOISILY ON Raymond Beddell's nightstand. "What?"

"Ray, it's Rooster. Lester was shot tonight."

"It's four fucking o'clock. What are you talking about?"

"Lester Smith was shot in the wrist while making a deal. My source at the police told me just a few minutes ago. That makes two dealers down this week. What the fuck is going on? Everybody is getting scared."

"Shut up! Lemme think. Okay. Call Sal and let's meet at Voogie's Coffee shop in an hour."

He hung up. *SONOFABITCH! First, "Demon" and Jimmy get the shit beat out of them and their legs cut, and now two of my best night dealers get beat up and shot. What the fuck is going on?"*

Ray Beddell met his two lieutenants at Voogie's. "So, wadda you two guys have on this? Are we being attacked by somebody from Chicago trying to grab our territory?"

Sal answered first, "I dunno about any invasions, boss, but one of our guys had the shit beat out of him and the other shot by a sniper, or so everybody thinks. Those assholes in Chicago aren't sneaky like that. Both of our boys had guns, but never had a chance to use them. I think this is somebody local."

"Yeah. Sal's right, but the only thing we know is that somebody big and strong fucked up "Demon" and Jimmy pretty good. They never got a look at the face because it was masked. The voice sounded like a girl, they said. A fucking girl! No girl could have fucked up those two," Rooster said.

"Well, we can't afford to lose any more of our boys. With Jimmy and "Demon" still on crutches, our revenue is dropping like a rock. The boss up in Gary is getting pissed. We better solve this or we're gonna be out of business. And you know what that means. Start putting an extra guard on the street guys. You two assholes start going to the parties. We need the big bucks from the rich kids. We don't have a lotta time. Now, go!"

The meeting broke up and Rooster and Sal tried to figure out who they were going to get to guard the four remaining street dealers. "I'll go up to the campus and look for party notices," Rooster said. "You go ask the street kids if they know anybody who wants to earn a few bucks covering the asses of our dealers."

"Yeah. Okay. I hope this works. I don't wanna have to go back to work for my uncle."

"It shouldn't be your uncle you're worried about. It should be the Gary boss and his errand boys. I hear they're not too gentle."

Rooster Lock wrote down two after-school parties coming up before the Thanksgiving break. These would probably be the last ones for the college kids before finals. He figured they had better score big this time. They'd been talking about expanding the inventory to include some of the opioids they could get their hands on along with some fentanyl. Selling these pills along with the usual stuff like ecstasy, meth, weed and coke, should bring in some serious bucks, and they needed big sales to make up for the lost money. The street traffic had slowed down a lot since the word got out that the dealers were being hit by an unknown assailant. Everybody was a little jumpy.

Sonya Keller noticed the party announcements too. She planned to attend and maybe do more disrupting. Around ten o'clock on the last Saturday before finals, she ensconced herself in a corner at one of those parties being thrown in a very nice, two-story brownstone in the best part of Gastonburg. The adult proctors were out of town, so the students took over and threw a party. She watched most of the people moving in, out and around the inside of the large house rented out to GJC students where the party was taking place. Around nine-thirty Rooster Lock walked in, the last of the three rapists who held that special place in her mind. His brick red, wiry hair stood straight up giving his nickname credence. Suppressing the rage she felt when she saw Rooster was very difficult for Sonya. After she cooled down some, she planned a "special experience" for Mr. Lock. His life was about to change permanently this evening... if he survived.

After an hour of dealing, Rooster grabbed a beer out of a cooler and sat down to relax. Sonya got up and walked slowly by him making sure he got a good look at her well-rounded butt stretching the yoga pants to the limit. She could feel his eyes following her, so she stole a quick glance over her shoulder and gave him a small, come-hither smile. He didn't seem to recognize her. And why should he? The last time he saw her, she was just barely seventeen, scrawny and had long hair. He was stoned out of his mind then too, so there was no way he knew the identity of the sexy-looking woman walking by.

As she expected, Rooster followed her out of the house and down the sidewalk. He caught up with her and started making small talk. "Walk with me for a little while," she said not looking at him. Rooster was clearly captivated by what he could see of Sonya's beautiful face and perfect curves. Along the way, they chatted about small things including the party they just left. She took care to not let Rooster see her full face head on. "So, what were you dealing in there, uh, Rooster?"

"Oh, not much. Just the usual stuff that college kids want while they're escaping from mommy and daddy. Do you want something? I can let you have a taste for free... if you know what I mean?"

"I DO know what you mean." By now they had turned a corner close to Sonya's parked car. There was an alley between back-to-back houses that looked pitch dark. "Let's go in here out of the light."

Rooster followed Sonya dutifully into the dark alley expecting some sexual favor, whereupon he was met with a sharp elbow right on his nose, blinding him with pain. She donned her "working gloves" and pulled her face mask up from her collar. Sonya could see his silhouette against the background lighting from the street shining down the alley. With a flurry of blows and kicks, she had Rooster on the ground trying to cover up from the beating he was getting. Sonya directed her sharpest blows at his kidneys and face. Ribs broke with cracking sounds. In seconds he was a bloody, gurgling mess moving in and out of consciousness. She paused to rest. "Who the fuck are you?" Rooster managed to mumble from his broken lips and jaw.

"I'm the angel of justice as far as you and your kind are concerned. Justice to me is seeing you assholes and your soul-destroying drug business out of my town, out of our lives. I won't quit picking you bastards off one at a time, until you're all gone. And please don't talk to me about what kids want. Of course they want drugs. It's what shitheads like you told them they wanted for years. They're parents are fucked up from drugs too. But you, Rooster, are not gonna deal drugs in my town again. You've been at it a long time, and you're gonna pay for the lives you helped destroy with a badly broken body and long jail time too. One of you bastards destroys hundreds of others. So, by eliminating you, justice is served."

Rooster made the mistake of trying to get up. His attempts were met with even stronger blows to vital areas including his groin. He was virtually helpless and barely conscious. She could have killed him in an instant, but she wanted to send yet another message to the network: *it's coming apart for you guys. You're going to pay a price you can't afford.* Sonya grabbed Rooster by the belt, lifted him bodily up as if he was a suitcase and hauled him out into the street where she deposited him in the street under a streetlight for all passers-by to see. Having surveilled the area beforehand, she knew there were no CCTV cameras here. She moved quickly into her car and drove off without lights for a couple blocks. She pulled over, removed the license plate screens and drove home as if nothing had happened.

"What the fuck do you mean, it was a girl?" Ray asked.

Through swollen lips and jaw, Rooster kept mumbling, "She said she was the angel of justice. She just kept hitting me. I never saw it coming. That bitch was as tall as me and STRONG!" Rooster said, groaning. "She picked me up with one hand and carried me bodily into the street. Man, I hurt all over. They told me that I'm pissing blood."

A passer-by saw Rooster's disheveled and broken body lying in the street and called the police. They, in turn, called for an ambulance. The EMTs peeled Rooster off the street and drove him to the hospital. The police did notice, however, that many packets of various drugs had spilled out of and were still in Mr. Lock's pockets. They processed his ID while the hospital tried to stop the bleeding and sew up his many cuts. They discovered, the way Sonya had intended, that Kevin "Rooster" Lock was a convicted felon on parole. Detectives hurried over to the hospital and put him under arrest and cuffed him to his hospital bed. It was highly unlikely that Mr. Lock would be going anywhere soon, but it was still protocol.

Ray Beddell was allowed to talk to Rooster, but only with an officer present. He was also notified that he was now a person of interest. What with his "stolen" van being involved in drug trafficking and now Rooster's problems, he was made to feel the heat too. Ray left without saying goodbye and went back home. While driving, he dialed up his main distribution boss in Gary. He told him the story about a vigilante girl taking out his supply network. He asked for help. The boss said he'd call him back. This was getting to be a little more than Ray could handle, and he was losing his network quickly. He was down to four street kids and Sal. That wouldn't cut it. For the first time in years, Ray Beddell felt scared. Not just worried but scared that he might be the next victim of the "angel of justice", or some Gary thug who came down here to rub him out. The sweat rolling down Ray Beddell's forehead got in his eyes and blinded him temporarily just as the low sun came out from behind a cloud. After furious blinking and rubbing, he looked up to see a human silhouette right in front of his car that was traveling 10 miles an hour too fast. The silhouette turned out to be an old woman crossing the street. He had just hit the brakes, but his momentum was enough to strike the woman and flip her over the hood of his BMW where she landed hard, staring at him through his windshield with dead eyes.

The morning paper described the accident naming Raymond Beddell as being arrested for vehicular homicide, speeding and failure to yield to a pedestrian. The police forensic team was gathering evidence while Ray's lawyer tried to bail him out of jail. Sonya read that report with more than a little satisfaction. The paper said Beddell was coming back from the hospital where one of his employees, a convicted felon, was being treated for multiple injuries, while himself being arrested for various drug crimes. *Hmm. Two for one? Maybe this "angel of justice" thing is doing some good in old Gastonburg?*

Sonya felt that she had accomplished much with the local drug kingpin now in jail for vehicular homicide and his network lieutenants in hospital for various physical problems that would keep them off the streets for a long time. Only Sal was left to deal with. She would follow him around to see what he was up to. She was certain that Sal had talked to Rooster and that her cover at the parties was blown. In order to put Sal out of commission, she'd have to be even more stealthy. Surprise was still her best asset even though she had superior physical strength and quickness to most men. But Sal was also large and muscular. He could pose a problem if Sonya didn't hit him in a vital area and he was able to recover from a lesser blow.

She watched Sal come and go from his apartment a few times. He stayed quite close to home most of the time. She noted that he didn't go to bars or hang out anywhere except the gym where he conducted 2-hour workouts five times per week. He took his exercise during the day and spent most evenings at home. On one particular evening, Sal traveled down into drug alley to check on his crew, or what was left of it. Sonya had been watching the area too, and when she saw Sal's bright orange muscle car pull up to a curb, she saw an opportunity.

As Sal emerged from one of the alleys, Sonya tripped him and instead of Sal falling on his face, he merely stumbled, turned and threw a roundhouse right fist at Sonya. He caught *her* by surprise and sent her tumbling to the ground. He was on her in a flash and she had to call on all her skills to fight him off. Sal got her briefly in a head lock, but a few well-directed defensive blows loosened his grip enough where she was able to escape. Without hesitation, she drilled a straight hand into his throat, and he collapsed gasping. She noticed movement from her left and saw the kid dealer and his bodyguard coming after her with guns drawn.

This was no time to be that heroic, and she took off running. The two kids chased her for a few meters firing their pistols. One round zipped by Sonya's ear and made her duck. But now she was around a corner and running like the wind. She kept running until she was clear of the area. Fortunately, she had the foresight to park several blocks away. As she slowed, she felt a throbbing on the left side of her face where Sal's glancing blow had knocked her down. She became angry, then embarrassed at having allowed herself to be struck by a thug. She found her car and drove home. Putting ice on the facial bruise didn't quell her anger or her shame.

Chapter 17

DEREK AND SONYA, PART II

DEREK AND SONYA HAD BEEN texting and calling several times a week since Derek went to Muncie. Sonya even learned how to use *Skype* with the computer upgrade her mom bought for her. Their friendship became more intimate during these increasingly personal conversations, and Sonya's inherent fear of men was subsiding to the point where she actually felt desire for the guy she now called her boyfriend. He was always very sweet to her, never chided her for anything, teased her about various things and otherwise continued a relaxed charm directed at her and them. She always looked forward to and returned his texts and calls. She did, however, keep her clandestine activities off the table of conversation. She knew she would have to tell him her story, but would it be before or after they made love for the first time? She decided that it would have to be before. It was sure to be their first major test as a couple, so she made the decision to be up-front before they went too far down the road of intimacy and trust. She was worried about telling him of her attacks on the drug dealers, however. These attacks were SO different from everything he now knew about her that she wasn't sure she'd found a way to tell him and justify her attitude without fearing losing Derek. She knew Derek was quite taken aback by her physical prowess and that incident at the baseball game parking lot demonstrated her ability to really harm someone. Actually, she rather feared scaring him off. He had to know about the trauma she experienced first so that he would understand her motives for doing the other things and taking the law into her own hands. She felt the growing need to be treated like a loved woman instead of just a good date or, if things progressed, a sexual object. She'd already been down that road, and it was repulsive in the extreme. Derek was winning her heart, and that was a good thing. Now, she had to take the necessary precautions to hold on to that precious dynamic.

WHILE PRACTICING WITH THE VARSITY at Ball State, Derek Murphy badly sprained his ankle and could not play in the Thanksgiving break tournament in Dayton, Ohio. He drove home Wednesday after his last class still wearing the plastic boot that kept him from aggravating his sprain. After settling in, and greeting his mom, he called Sonya and she hurried over to see him. This would also be the first time she'd meet his mother.

Grace Murphy was a tall, blonde, fair-skinned woman in her late 30s. She had pale blue eyes and wheat-colored hair. She eyed Sonya appraisingly being somewhat surprised at her height and physical build. "You certainly are as beautiful as Derek has said you are, but I didn't expect someone as big."

"I'm a late bloomer," was all Sonya could think of saying while blushing deeply.

"Well, Derek can't stop talking about you, and I trust his judgement. Let's have some tea."

The three of them sat around a small table enjoying a cup of hot, steaming tea on this chilly Indiana evening. The conversation swirled around everybody's jobs and studies. Derek was taking three classes and enjoying them. Grace insisted that Derek do well in school so he wouldn't be always struggling with work and money like she was. Clearly, the basketball scholarship was the only way Derek could get a 4-year degree and avoid the crushing student debt that state and Federal Governments imposed, stupidly, on people they knew would have trouble paying them back. Everyone agreed that it was a kind of indentured servitude not unlike that imposed on crooks and miscreants exported to the New World from England in the 17th and 18th centuries.

Grace Murphy worked as a shipping clerk at a local warehouse making enough to pay the rent on their small apartment and feeding her son and herself decently. Her family background was rather typical for a blue-collar, upper mid-west family at the time she came along. She made friends easily, but never met any boys in her high school that interested her. They were mostly interested in her good looks and how quickly she would drop her knickers for them. She ended that fantasy by not dating any of them or, for that matter, giving them the time of day. Then, along came Andrew Poindexter. He played basketball at the high school the next town closer to Chicago. Andy was over 6 feet tall, with rich, medium brown skin color. He was very handsome and had a chatter that made the girls laugh and feel comfortable around him. After one of the games between their two schools, Grace was cleaning up the concession stand where she worked for a few dollars. Andrew hustled her easily. She gave him her phone number and they started dating… away from Gastonburg. Andrew had a car and would meet her at remote places, pick her up and away they would go.

Andrew Poindexter was a gentle, attentive lover and Grace fell deeply in love with him even before she graduated from high school. They were married and moved to Chicago a month after she graduated. Andrew had graduated a year before and was employed in the windy city. Derek was born barely a year later, and Grace's time was now split between her waitressing job and her son.

Andrew, however, didn't adapt well to this domestic turn in his life. He had met some men at his factory who played the games of gambling, women and booze. Soon, Andrew came home later and later – even on work nights.

Grace was able to smell the liquor and perfume on him when he walked in, undressed and fell into bed. He never really tried to hide his "player" persona from her.

After a few years of this embarrassing situation, with Derek beginning to grow into adolescence, Andrew Poindexter disappeared. Missing person's reports yielded nothing. To the Chicago authorities, he was just another player who got himself jammed up and was taken out of the "scene" one way or another. The stack of unsolved missing person's cases in that city grew almost daily. Andrew Poindexter was simply gone.

After a couple of cups of tea and with the conversation having run most of its course, Sonya offered to take everyone to a movie. Even though Derek could drive – his boot being on his left ankle – Sonya volunteered to make it easy on him and would drive everyone to the show. Grace said she hadn't been to a movie in years. Off they went. With the money Sonya was saving up from her job at Ned's studio, she sprang for the whole movie, popcorn and sodas. In the theater, Derek found himself wedged between his mother and Sonya. The young lovers managed to find a way to hold hands. Grace cast a couple of furtive glances their way and smiled, knowing that her boy was happy and possibly in love. Sonya seemed like just the kind of girl that Derek should be around.

When they returned from the movies, the three of them chatted for a little while, then Grace excused herself and went to bed. Sonya and Derek snuggled on the couch with the TV on quietly. *Well, this is as good a time as any to tell him.*

"I really like your mom," Sonya said. "Are you guys going to have a nice T-day with her parents and others?"

"Yeah. Her parents and sisters are throwing a big dinner. I didn't think to invite you not knowing what your situation is completely. Sorry."

"Not to worry. Maybe next year, or at the Christmas break..."

"Okay."

"Derek, I'm really enjoying you and am learning to trust you. You have been very consistent, gentle and good to me every time we've been together. I'd like things to continue."

"I feel the same about being with you. I want to spend a lot more time with you whenever I can."

"Good. But now is the time for me to tell you my story about how I am the way I am. You wondered why somebody like me has led such a sheltered life. Well, here's the story."

Sonya proceeded to tell him how her upbringing was such a disaster and the reasons for her being very untrusting of men and very insecure within her own skin. She told him about the beatings and the rapes encouraged by her own father and Erica's husband. She spared no details. She also told him about how the changes in her physicality were among the first steps toward renewing her personal confidence. She told him about how Kelsey virtually saved her life, and how Ned taught her how to take care of herself. To say the least, Derek was more than a little shocked, but instead of being angry, he had tears in his eyes and on his cheeks. "Why are you crying?"

"I hurt because you were hurt so badly. It hurts me to know that the woman I'm falling in love with had to endure such horrible things. That said, I'm equally impressed that you've hauled yourself up from that pit of hurt and despair in your life. Your poor mother... How did she handle all this?" he asked wiping away the tears.

"She basically ran for her life too. I think the battered wives' clinic helped her talk through the pain. Even though Mom is a very tough person, she's still pretty twitchy about men, and who can blame her?"

"No kidding. What does she think about us dating?"

"She likes you and has come to trust me in all things. Now here is the other part of the story."

Sonya proceeded to give Derek a brief sketch of her acts of retribution against her father and his friends without directly implicating herself, thus giving him deniability. Maybe at some other point she would address how poorly she thought the authorities handle the death-dealing drug trade and the associated organized crime that fosters it. Maybe. Someday. But not this day.

Derek swept her into his arms and held her for minutes. He just wanted to feel her body next to his. This beautiful woman had opened up to him in ways he never expected from any woman. Then, *this* woman was special in every way he knew, and, he suspected, in ways he didn't yet know. He was drawn to her more each day. Maybe this is what falling in love, ass-end over tea kettles, felt like. He was sure to know before long.

For the first time in her life, Sonya Keller felt secure in the arms of a man not named Ned Morrow. It was like she felt Derek Murphy pouring his heart and soul into her own heart and soul. They kissed and hugged. They kissed some more. Derek moved his hands across her entire body, and she let him. *This must be the moment Kelsey was talking about.* She felt real arousal for the first time, too. She felt she was ready to make real love with this man, but not tonight. It would have to be more private. Derek was back to school in a day or two and having sex now only to have her lover leave right away didn't seem right.

After a few more minutes of shared affection and passion, Sonya got up off the couch and walked around. She smiled at Derek and fanned her face with her hands. "I've never felt THAT before. I liked it. Thank you for being gentle and patient. Now that you know what I've been through, it looks like you understand that my pace toward lovemaking is different than yours... I guess."

"Well, I do want to make love with you, but not until you're ready and that you think the time and place are right. I get all the other stuff. I'm terribly sorry and hurt by your story; hurt because you hurt. It's awful that you now have to carry the burden and the anger and all the other stuff because of those guys and the drug culture that created them. I hope those people being punished helped relieve some of the pressure and stress brought on by your anger and humiliation. What can I do to make it better for you?"

"Just keep doing what you're doing. If we need a place to vent our physical needs and emotions, there's always the handball court." They both laughed as the tension broke from her wise crack.

"Yeah. That should do it. I know it won't be long before you're kicking my ass at that too."

"What else have I done that kicked your ass?"

"You made me fall in love. I guess. I've never been this close to someone and felt I didn't have to prove anything. I'm just being myself around a woman for the first time. Yes, I've had girlfriends before, but not like you. Nobody I've ever known or even heard of is like you. Let's just keep letting this grow... if you're willing?"

"Oh, I'm willing. Right now, I'd better get home. I'll call you tomorrow when I wake up."

The short drive home was filled with mental delights. Sonya had trouble focusing on driving and almost ran a red light. A car zooming past in the cross street reminded her to pay attention. *Focus, girl. Get home safely. Dream about your boyfriend later... when it's safer.*

Sonya called Derek on Thanksgiving morning to chat. He was helping his mom prepare the dish they had to take to the dinner. She was also helping Erica with a pie. Sonya and Erica were invited over to the Morrows' where their relatives would join them for the celebration. They all shared what they were thankful for this day, and as Sonya told how thankful she was for the Morrows being her refuge, her love family and her life coaches, tears streamed down her face. It was an emotional scene for everyone, but everyone also felt safe in sharing their emotions and their love. Giving thanks almost seemed redundant to the fact that Sonya and the Morrows were so deeply entwined. Erica was equally grateful for the Morrows giving

Sonya what she needed and when she needed it, things she couldn't provide due to the circumstances nobody brought up.

When the dinner ended, everyone pitched in with the clean-up, made leftover plates, ate pie and drank coffee. Sonya and Erica went home and, with full stomachs, went to bed to sleep the sleep of the contented and the loved.

Derek stopped by that next Friday morning to pick Sonya up and went out for coffee and a chat. They each described their previous day and just enjoyed the company of one another. The day was sunny and not that cold, so they walked slowly around the park where Sonya had once dismantled her father. Derek clumped along with his boot, so the pace was leisurely. There were just a few strollers and some kids playing touch football, a most Norman Rockwell-like scene of middle America. They held hands as they walked and just enjoyed a warm, loving afternoon. Derek had to leave in the morning, sprained ankle and all, for an afternoon team meeting. She walked him back to his car and he drove her home. They parked in the lot next to the apartments and kissed and looked into each other's eyes with longing. Sonya reluctantly pushed herself away, and assured Derek that she would be here waiting for him whenever he could get home. "I guess that means we're going steady," Derek said.

"Yeah. I'm good with that. I don't need any more complications or distractions. I'm glad you're with me even when you're away." She kissed him again and was out the door. As she ran up the stairs, she turned and waved, smiling. *I can't remember being this happy.*

Chapter 18

The Winter of Contentment and Danger

"Mom, I think it's time I had my own place. Are you okay with that?"

"I was wondering how long it would be after you met that nice boy that you'd be looking for a little more, uh, privacy," Erica said. Her deadpan gave way to a shy smile

"Does that mean you don't mind?"

"Do you think you can find a place nearby?"

"I've actually been looking at a duplex about two blocks over, next to the grocery store."

"Can you afford it?"

"Well, it's got a nice, roomy studio above one of the regular apartments. They're asking $300 per month. So, yes, I can afford it. Ned's paying me $15.00 per hour now, so I've been able to stash some money for the deposit and whatnot."

"So, my girl has been doing her homework, I see. Good for you. I'm proud of you. You're just twenty-one, so you should be on your own. The firm is paying me good money now, so I can afford you not helping. You wouldn't mind cooking me a couple dinners a week, though, would you?"

"No. Of course not. So, you're okay with me moving into my own place?"

"Yes. Take me over to it and let me see what you've turned up."

Meanwhile, at Gastonburg police headquarters, a detective named Abel Baker was going through some police reports related to some violence directed against suspected and actual drug dealers. After interrogating Raymond Beddell about his visit with "Rooster" Lock, an unusual pattern started developing in his mind. Lock kept saying that a large girl he tried to pick up at a party beat the shit out of him. So, why was Beddell so interested in Lock? While the detective couldn't prove it, Beddell, with his shiny car, ponytail and diamond rings profiled as a second-tier drug dealer. Beddell's lawyer just got him bailed out on the traffic charges, and since he had no priors, the judge granted bail at something like $10,000. He was assigned an ankle monitor, because of the potential flight risk.

Then there were these other reports that showed severe body damage to the two guys who were using a vehicle registered to Beddell. They were caught holding significant drug weight and would spend serious time in jail. Their sliced Achilles tendons added to the mystery. They also said that their attacker sounded like a girl, but the attacker's face was covered and just appeared from "nowhere", again beating the shit out of these guys before cutting them. Then there were the two street dealers, one being badly beaten and dumped in the street in cable tie cuffs, and the other apparently shot by a sniper.

Baker's partner, Howard Schmidt, was pawing through another stack of reports concerning drug crimes and violent outcomes in Gastonburg when he came upon a report that talked about a large female cutting one guy's hand off and slicing another up pretty badly. Then, there was this really sorry loser, Cromwell Keller, who had several bones broken while in the park one night a couple years ago. He reported never seeing anything but a large, dark silhouette come out of the shadows before his lights went out.

"Let's get a coffee, Howie," said Baker. "We might have ourselves a vigilante out there somewhere. We'd better start finding out about that."

They chatted for a while and tried to create a profile of an attacker that obviously knew what they were doing. But the sniping incident was puzzling, as were the reports that perhaps a large female with great strength and skill was attacking a drug ring, probably led by this asshole Beddell. "Maybe we should start looking into physical fitness or martial arts businesses to see if anyone fitting this description pops up," said Schmidt.

"Good idea. Let me start with the martial arts places. The guy who lost his hand said that all he saw was the flash of what might have been a sword. Jesus! What do we have on our hands, here? A fucking *ninja*?"

Abel Baker was a 20-year veteran of the Gastonburg police department. He joined right after mustering out of the U.S. Marine Corps. He tried to keep in shape, but the desk work kept him out of the gym by absorbing his "free" time. His physical profile kept slipping south into his waist. He was balding, but still not fifty years old. He had sparkling blue eyes that darted about all the time as if he were looking for someone to pop out of a wall and attack him. A lengthy tour in Iraq would do that to a guy.

Howard Schmidt was a lifelong Gastonburg policeman. He went from high school right into the police academy. From there, he donned the dark blue patrolman's uniform and stayed in it for 20 years. At age thirty-nine he applied for the detective squad. He never could gain weight no matter how many milkshakes he drank, which pissed off his partner, Baker every day. Schmidt was dark-complected and took a lot of needling about his family's close relationship with a woodpile and all the bad jokes that went with it. Nonetheless, Howard Schmidt was a tireless and persistent investigator and had brought many old, unsolved cases to light where criminals were found even in faraway states and prosecuted successfully.

Abel Baker found himself coming into the martial arts studio of Ned Morrow a week before Christmas. No classes were going on at the time, but a quite muscular, tall woman was pumping some serious looking iron in the gym. She saw Baker, grabbed a towel and asked, "May I help you?"

"I hope so. My name is Detective Abel Baker from the Gastonburg P.D." He flashed his badge and I.D. "Who might you be?"

"I'm Sonya Keller. What can I do for you?"

"Do you know Cromwell Keller? Any relation?"

"Yeah. I knew him. He's my father. Isn't he still in jail?"

"Oh yeah. How would you say your relationship with your father was or is?"

"We didn't have one. After he refereed having his friends rape my mother and I, we filed a bunch of restraining orders for him to stay away from us."

"Okay. So, what happened after he got out of jail for allegedly beating your mother and possessing all that dope?"

"He found out where we lived and nearly beat my mother to death."

"Did you know that not long after, somebody beat HIM almost to death?"

"Yeah. I heard it on the news."

"And you wouldn't know anything about that night, would you?"

"As I told the policemen who came to our house the next day, I was visiting my girlfriend and then took my nightly run. So, no. I don't know anything more than what I heard on the news. That was almost 2 years ago, wasn't it?"

"Yeah just a month longer.

"Say, you look pretty strong. How much do you lift?"

"I don't really pay attention. I just try to stay in shape so I can teach my classes. I teach self-defense classes for men and women."

"Really? Are you qualified?"

"Yes." She pointed to the wall displaying her certificates and her belt achievements. "Why all the questions?"

"Well, it seems that a bunch of thugs that we've arrested over the last couple years keep saying they were attacked by a large, shadowy figure that talked like a woman. They say she was about 6 feet tall and really, really strong. How tall are you, Ms. Keller?"

"Just a little over 6 feet. I grew almost an inch last year. For your information, I weighed myself this morning and was just a little under 175 pounds."

"Do you own or possess those fighting swords?"

"Yes. My teacher gave me a set for graduating high school and achieving my first black belt in karate."

"I may want to look at them and have them tested someday. You can see my concern about somebody acting as a vigilante, can't you? We frown on that sort of thing. Don't get me wrong. The people who were badly hurt probably deserved every bit of it, but it's still against the law for a private citizen to take the law into their own hands. Do you understand?"

"Perfectly."

"Okay. Just know that somebody like you sort of fits the preliminary profile for this vigilante-ism, so I'm telling you that you are now a person of interest. What that means is that we will continue to investigate these crimes and activities, and if any more evidence emerges or these events keep occurring, we'll be taking a much closer look at your activities. So, if you know of anybody who might be seeking revenge or retribution against a drug ring, be sure to let me know. Here's my card, Ms. Keller. Have a good day."

Baker returned to his office and found Schmidt waiting for him. "Anything?"

"Naw. Nobody knows anyone fitting that description that we put together. You?"

"Yep. I met Cromwell Keller's daughter, the one who was sexually abused as a teenager. Remember him... and her? She is one specimen of womanhood. Before she saw me come into Ned Morrow's studio, she was benching at least two-hundred pounds... like it was nothing. She's also a multiple black belt in *karate, judo* and has one in *kendo* too."

"What's *kendo*?"

"That's Japanese sword fighting. Don't you know anything?"

"Oh. Is that where they cut each other to pieces with a two-handed sword?"

"Yes. Here's that report about those three punks who kept trying to mug people for drug money. One of the kids was holding a knife on this large, shadowy figure who sounded like a girl. Next thing he knew his hand was on the ground and his buddy almost got sliced open. They said it happened in a flash."

"Holy shit, Baker. Do we have any proof at all connecting this woman to these crimes?"

"Nope. No CCTV footage. No DNA. No prints. Nada. She didn't even flinch when I mentioned all the details either. She's a cool customer."

* * * * *

DURING THE WEEK BEFORE CHRISTMAS break, Sonya moved into her first studio apartment. When Derek came home, still wearing the boot on his ankle, she had him over to see the place and make him a dinner. Sonya had decided that she was going to let things develop naturally and see how well her instincts guided her. She wore her most feminine outfit and even put on a little make-up and lipstick. She made her favorite dish, broiled lemon-pepper chicken with a big salad and freshly baked rolls. The oven and stove in her flat were adequate and worked perfectly.

Derek was late. But he limped in, apologized, removed his boot and shook the newly fallen snow off his jacket. He wore a midnight blue bulky sweater, blue jeans and a big smile that made his dimples deeper and his eyes brighter than ever... at least that's how Sonya perceived them. He even brought a nice bottle of wine. Sonya kissed him hello and told him to sit while she opened the wine and served up the dinner. As she had learned from cooking for her mother, timing was everything, and this dinner came together perfectly. They ate, drank, laughed and chatted as if they'd been doing this for years. The sharing of intimacy from their last encounter had clearly allowed for a much more comfortable atmosphere.

Derek helped her clear the table after dessert, a simple bowl of butter-pecan ice cream. Her dish set and flatware came directly from the local discount superstore but had pretty designs and served the purposes for which they were intended. She rinsed and stacked the dishes in the dishwasher and turned it on. "Help me pick out some music," she asked.

"WELL, LET'S SEE WHAT YOU have." He looked at her small CD collection and picked out an oldie, Dionne Warwick's Greatest Hits. "Where did you get this?"

"Oh, my mom bought it a couple years ago when we first moved into our place. I liked it, so I bought a copy for myself." The smooth, easy listening was a perfect mood setter. "Can you dance?"

"Yeah, I can limp around some." He took her in his arms and felt her strong body relax against him. He held her close and they swayed to the plaintive strains of one of the ballads. "You are a delight to hold, Sonya."

"I've never been held like this before. It feels like we've been dancing together for years."

After the song ended, she said, "Let me get the wine."

Derek sat on the couch waiting for her to bring the glasses filled with the chilled Moselle. The couch was one of those convertible types that unhinged and laid out to be a queen-sized bed. There was a lever on the side that released the back of the couch. It was comfortable and roomy in the upright position, so Derek stretched his legs.

"Comfy?"

"I am. How do you like the wine?"

"It's delicious. What should we toast to?"

"Why not just toast us and a beautiful evening together?"

"That's the best idea so far. By the way, how did you like the chicken?"

"It was delicious too. You noticed that I didn't look for your pet dog to feed it to, didn't you?"

"Wise ass. You know I don't have a dog." They both snickered at that. Sonya, balancing her wineglass, leaned over and kissed him slowly and sweetly. She felt she was getting the hang of this and Derek had such a kissable mouth. That's what Kelsey told her too, and she was continuing to confirm that thesis with first-hand knowledge.

Soon, the wine was finished, and the healthy young couple were in each other's arms kissing deeply and feeling the swoon of lovemaking overtake them. Derek took the lead in this activity and slowly led Sonya to a place of no return. Clothes came off, longing looks persisted as hands moved here and there. Then there came the moment when Sonya reached for the release lever and the back of the couch suddenly fell back with the entwined couple going with it. "I think we just fell for each other," Derek said huskily.

"That's a pretty lame and corny line if I ever heard one," she said back while clinging more tightly to his nakedness with her own.

The lovemaking was tender, slow and gentle as Derek tried to sense how Sonya would handle this intimacy. She went with his lead and discovered a physical enjoyment that was ever so different than the physical release of martial arts, running or lifting weights. She let her mind go as her body responded so perfectly to Derek's moves and care. *So, this is what it's supposed to be like. It's just a matter of finding the right lover. The real deal is a good thing. No wonder so many people do so many things to get to this place.*

Later, after both lovers were spent from the physical mindlessness of climaxes, Sonya got up and extracted a comforter from the closet. She wrapped them both up in it and snuggled in Derek's arms. "Thank you for introducing me to real sex the way, I guess, it should be enjoyed."

"I wouldn't do anything else with you. You are a precious woman, Sonya

Keller. I'm just doing what I can to ensure that the part of you that you've never experienced before was done right. Do you feel loved?"

"I do, if that's what this is all about. If being held and treated like a real person is what you meant to do, it worked. I think I even had an, uh, orgasm."

"Well, that's a good thing, isn't it?"

"Oh yes!" she said smiling into his neck. "It's a very good thing."

They were silent for a while and just enjoyed listening to the album sing to them. Then, Sonya said, "You know, the story I told you over Thanksgiving about what I did is somehow not completely satisfying. Even though I exacted my revenge on the people who hurt me and my mom, there's still a hole in my... heart, for want of a better place, that needs filling. It's like I feel I need to do something good. All this power and strength is just being sort of wasted on really bad people, and I might end up getting in real trouble. So, I've got to figure out a way to use what I have to make something good happen to myself, for my friends and maybe even something bigger. These thoughts have been bugging me a lot more lately, and I'd like to figure out what the hell I'm doing with my life. Being with you brings this sense of unfulfilled purpose out much stronger."

"Well, that's some pretty heavy stuff. Where do I fit into all that?"

"Yeah. Well, I think you've convinced me that all men are not drooling rapists and drug addicts." They laughed and Derek emitted a mock sigh of relief.

"So, how's that history class going? Are you learning things that might add to your 'new' mission in life?"

"Maybe. My classmate, Butch, wants to be a cop. He's made me think of doing something like that too. God, I have SO much to learn! I just can't go around busting heads all my life for just my own satisfaction and purging my own demons. What happens when all that selfishness goes away?"

"It sounds like it already is. Maybe tonight created more change in your life than just you and me discovering each other's bodies and doing what comes naturally."

"You may be right." With that, she unwrapped herself from the blanket and stood in the center of the living area completely naked. The Warwick album had finished, and she bent over to put something else in. It was a blues guitar album by a long-dead artist. It never got much playing time on the radio but was a brilliant display of his true talents and away from the mainstream commercial stuff that made him famous. She then stood back up, turned around and proceeded to go through a series of punches, kicks and other martial arts power moves. She put on a show that had Derek sitting there fascinated and amazed at the incredible beauty of Sonya's naked form, its agility, the muscular definition and the real grace she exhibited. "You should see your face!" she said, controlling a laugh.

"Come here. There's something else I want to tell you." Her naked display had rekindled his desire and they once again joined in passionate lovemaking that now included Sonya taking a greater role. Derek felt that he had never been so aroused and taken by any woman or image of a woman in his life. He thought to himself, after they'd finished and were panting to regain their breath, *This is scary good. I better be very careful with this woman. She may end up commanding what I do with my life. But could that be so bad?*

Chapter 19

LOOSE ENDS

DURING THE CHRISTMAS OR WINTER break, Sonya and Derek continued their love affair and spent almost the entire time together. The Morrows threw a New Year's Eve party and invited Sonya, Erica, Derek and Grace to share the celebration of the new year. It was a lovely, joyous party with dancing, music, lots of finger food and minimal alcohol consumption. Kelsey brought a nice-looking, wild-haired young man to the party. This was the chemistry lab partner and tennis player she told Sonya about. They'd been dating quite steadily since. Erica and Grace spent some time getting better acquainted and talked about their children who were clearly in serious love with one another. At the stroke of midnight, everyone cheered, raised their glass of champagne and kissed everyone in sight. Derek and Sonya looked into each other's glistening eyes feeling that this would be the first of many happy new years to come. At about one-thirty, Sonya took Derek by the hand, grabbed their coats and slipped out the back door to her car. She drove directly to her studio flat where they rang in the new year with an especially intense and joyous lovemaking session.

New Year's Day dawned sunny and mild for northern Indiana in winter. Derek and Sonya decided to enjoy a nice, brisk walk to the park and back from her flat. Unseen was a dark blue BMW sedan parked near her studio apartment. "There she is," said Sal. "She's damn near as big as her boyfriend. I've been tracking her ever since I spotted her coming out of that karate studio. It has to be her. I've never seen any woman in this town that looks like that."

"Okay. Let's have a look and a chat with those two. Her boyfriend seems to be limping a little, so I'll hold him off while you deal with the bitch," said Ray. "Man. It's New Year's Day and we're doing this shit. The boss man said we don't have a day to lose. We'd better clean this up."

THE TWO DRUG DEALERS GOT out of the car and followed Derek and Sonya into the park. At first, they were oblivious to the pair of thugs stalking them, but Sonya caught the movement of two large shadows from the slanting sun and turned around. She saw Ray Beddell and Sal Palermo walking quickly toward them.

"Uh, oh! We have company."

Ray went right after Derek and pushed him up against a tree with a knife to his throat. Sal brought out a long K-Bar killing knife and started toward Sonya. She easily dodged his initial thrust and came to her "on-guard" position. "You're the bitch who's been attacking our guys, aren't you? Well, it's time you paid the price for fucking with us. Say goodbye to your boyfriend, because you're both about to be chopped meat."

He came at her again, and she attempted to disarm his knife hand with her best grab and spin move. But Sal was too strong and was ready for it, pulling free from her grasp. Once again he threatened her with the knife. This time, Sonya tried a leg sweep and was successful at bringing him down. She was on him in a flash, stomping his knife hand and aiming her next kick to his groin. She missed slightly but followed up with another kick to his face. Sal yelled and tried to cover up, but Sonya was quick enough to dodge his next blow. He lunged for the knife and that was his undoing. She kicked Sal in the side of his head sending him sprawling on the brown grass. He glared at her with dark, beady eyes and a snarl curled his lips. He jumped up and lunged for her with both hands. This, Sonya dodged easily, threw her leg into his and sent him sprawling again. This time, however, she dropped a knee into his back, knocking his wind out and cracking a couple ribs. Another sharp blow to his temple rendered Sal unconscious.

Sonya turned to see Ray still holding the knife to Derek's throat. "Don't come near me, bitch, or I'll cut his throat!" Sonya looked across the park and saw two Gastonburg policemen sprinting from the street. Ray took a glance in that direction and that's all Sonya needed to see. She had his knife hand behind his back in a second and shoved it up under his shoulder blade causing Ray to scream loudly. Derek jumped away from the tree and was told to hold still by the just-arriving police.

Breathlessly, Derek told them they were just attacked by these two guys. "We know. We saw the whole thing from the car. Are you two all right?"

"Yes. Thanks for being here," said Sonya.

"That's our job, lady. Man, you sure fucked this guy up." The other policeman not talking had Sal cuffed and rolled him over. He was groaning and looked like he was regaining his senses. "What did you two do to piss off these guys?"

"You'll have to ask them. They just jumped us. Maybe they mistook us for somebody else."

"Hey, Chip, this asshole with the ankle monitor is Raymond Beddell. Didn't we have him in the other day?"

"Yeah. He killed that old lady with his car. Out on bail. Oh yeah. I was the officer guarding that other scumbag Lock when this asshole was in talking to him about the girl he thought beat the shit out of him. Was that you, ma'am? Did you put his street dealer in the hospital? It looks like you could do it."

Sonya looked at him for a long second, then said, "Oh. Was that the guy who I beat up when he tried to rape me after a house party? I didn't report it, because it was no big deal."

"Well, he was pretty broken up. How did that happen?"

"Well, I teach self-defense classes at Ned Morrow's studio. I was just defending myself against an attack on my person. That guy, whoever he is, just picked the wrong girl to assault."

"I'll say. We've been watching these two knuckleheads for a long time. Violating bail with a deadly weapon will put this bag of shit away for a long time. No bail. This big guy... I don't know him. We'll see. Anyway, I'll need you to come to the station with us while I write up the report. We're calling in another wagon to haul these two to holding. Let's go."

Derek had a small nick on his neck and Sonya used her handkerchief to clean the few drops of blood. He looked at her with even more amazement. "I thought I was in real trouble. You're going to have to teach me how to do what you do. You seem to attract bad guys."

"Well, there are a lot of bad guys out there, sweetheart. I've told you about some of them. In this small town, they all probably know each other. I'll be happy to teach you some basic self-defense. Christ! New Year's Day... These fucking people are real animals."

Her use of the "F" word derivative made Derek raise his eyebrows and give her a side-long smile.

"What? You never heard a woman swear before? Man, I learned from the best... or in his case, the worst. Don't piss me off!" she said with mock seriousness. "Let's go with the cops and get this over with."

They arrived at the police station and sat with the officers and helped them finish their incident reports. They declined an offer for a ride home and walked the 2 miles to her studio apartment. There, they collapsed on the couch. After a little while, Sonya got up and poured each of them a stiff drink of bourbon. That seemed to quell their nerves a little and they soon fell asleep.

Derek woke about an hour later and slipped out from under Sonya's head.

She woke, however, and reached out for him. "I've gotta go pack and get ready for Bobby Clark to take me back to school. Our classes start tomorrow morning."

"Oh, crap. I forgot. My new class starts tomorrow too. Well, thanks for another stimulating day together. Between the sex and the violence, maybe we should sit down and write another bad movie script. The drug component is certainly implied." They both laughed, and Sonya drove Derek back to his apartment. She went in with him and talked with Grace while he packed. When he was finished, Sonya hugged Grace and kissed Derek goodbye. He said he would call once he got back to Muncie.

"Did you tell my mom what happened today?"

"Yeah, but I think she feels good about having me around to protect you from the bad guys," Sonya said.

"You bet I do, but who is going to protect him down in Muncie?" Grace added, smiling.

"I'll be fine, Mom. Don't worry," Derek chimed.

"Have a safe trip, darling. Talk to you soon." Sonya kissed him and was out the door.

A few days later, detectives Baker and Schmidt arrived together to visit Sonya at the studio. "Miss Keller. May we talk with you for a minute?" asked Baker.

"Sure. What now?"

"We just heard about your run-in with Beddell and his gorilla. How do they know you or you know them?" asked Schmidt.

"I don't know them. I don't know how they know me. Why are you asking me?"

Baker: "Well, they told us that they think you're the attacker who messed up their boys. Wadda you have to say about that?"

"I have nothing to say about that. I don't know them. What do they do? What's their problem with me?"

Schmidt: "Yeah. Well, we can trace the guys who were messed up and this knucklehead Beddell back to your father, Cromwell Keller. Apparently Beddell was your father's drug supplier, and the other three goons were the bag men. Would you know anything about that?"

"No. I stayed away from them when they were at the house. I never looked at them. I locked myself in my room until the day they all raped me and my mother. I can't ever remember this guy Beddell. I'm glad they're in jail, or whatever. Why shouldn't I be? But you already knew all that, didn't you? You read my mother's and my complaints and reports, didn't you?" she asked quizzically.

BAKER: "YES. OF COURSE. WE'RE very sorry for your experience. But we're trying to tie up some loose ends to these cases and the one dangling thread is that nobody knows who put these bad guys in the hospital. We were hoping you could shed some light on that. Any ideas?"

"Nope. With guys like that, something bad was bound to happen, right?"

Baker: "Yeah. Well, thanks for your time. We had to ask these questions."

Schmidt: "So, when are you going to try out for the Olympics? You look like you could win some medals in many events. How fast can you run? Have you ever thrown a javelin?"

"I've never competed in any sports except *karate* and *kendo*. I wouldn't have the first idea about all that other stuff. Why do you ask?"

Schmidt: "Well, I've never seen a woman built like you, and from the reports from the arresting officers you took care of Mr. Palermo in great style. You should be a world-class athlete. Ever think about that?"

"Is there anything else I can help you gentlemen with? I've got to get ready for my next class."

"Mind if we watch?"

"No. Sit over there in the corner. My students are just warming up."

The two detectives were awed by the skill, speed and patience Sonya had with the students. This was an advanced class in self-defense and some of the things Sonya was showing the students, the detectives had never seen before, not even in their police academy training. At the end of class, they told Sonya how impressed they were and thanked her for her cooperation. "We hope you lead a peaceful life, Miss Keller. Thanks again for helping us get some bad guys off the streets."

Once outside the studio, they looked up to see that snow was starting to fall. Schmidt said, "I'm sure she was the one who fucked up those knuckleheads. Did you see how she flipped that guy in there? Those assholes on the street didn't stand a chance."

"CAN'T PROVE A THING, THOUGH. No evidence. Lock said he could ID her face, but it was dark and at night. That'd never make it past the third question in court."

"Yeah. Well, we can just tell the lieutenant that we tied up the loose ends on this case."

"Yep. Let's go get a hot toddy somewhere. Happy New Year!"

Chapter 20

THE NEXT LEVEL

AS WINTER GAVE WAY TO spring in Gastonburg, Indiana, Sonya Keller kept teaching her classes at Ned's studio and stayed interested in Mr. Hullaby's second semester class on post-Civil War history. In it, Hullaby emphasized the role that race relations – or the lack of them – played in forming the social order in America. It was, to everyone's surprise, very unsettling and quite horrifying in many instances, especially with the emergence of the "robber barons" and their emphasis on class warfare. They were shocked and dismayed at how the waves of immigrants from Europe were treated so badly and how the internecine gang wars brought over from that continent were renewed on the streets of our cities. It always seemed that blood had to be spilled before anything worthwhile emerged. Again, as before in the previous semester, it was poverty that was the common denominator in America's struggle to perfect capitalism. And, as always, the white, Christian emphasis continued to look for scapegoats. If it weren't the Irish Catholics vs. the Protestants, it was something to do with the Jews.

As the class moved into the pre-WW II eras, it was the anti-Semitism that dominated foreign relations. The rise of the Third Reich in Germany found its scapegoat right from the beginning, the Jews. But the National Socialists

(Nazis) were also anti-communist. Ironically, the Russian communists were also anti-Semites. In fact, Czarist Russia conducted decades-long pogroms against the Jews in all the provinces including Ukraine.

One day, Sonya put her hand in the air and asked, "Why does everybody hate the Jews?"

Silence. Finally, Hullaby, with more than a little snark in his voice said, "Because they didn't fight back. They let it happen. Their persecution was allowed. But you can't blame the Jews entirely for this situation. They were the oppressed minority in every way you can imagine. It seems that the Christian churches needed a fall guy too. In America, the resurgence of southern white politics and the birth of the white southern Christian churches created yet another avenue of separation in order to justify its own righteousness. Blaming the Jews for getting Jesus killed was an easy thing to sell to the white people who still felt the sting of the Civil War and the subsequent oppression and exploitation by northern whites. They had put the black man back into "his place" by then, so they needed yet another target for their rage. This was all done in Jesus' name, mind you. Love thy neighbor... as long as he wasn't Jewish. Most sadly, the realization of their hypocrisy died among the pews and choir lofts of the southern church culture. When Jews were fleeing Europe in droves during the early 1930s, our government made their exodus to the United States extremely difficult. The mostly white, Christian politicians had constituents who said, "NO JEWS!" One of Roosevelt's appointees in the state department, named Breckenridge Long, created a very special bureaucracy that created enough red tape to bind the emigration of Jews into Gordian knots that were never untied. Ships filled with Jewish refugees were refused ports along our eastern seaboard – and especially in the southern states – so that the passengers were forced to return to Europe or starve aboard those ships. So, yeah. We Americans have much to answer for too. Things improved greatly after the discovery of the death camps in Eastern Europe after they were "liberated" by allied forces. Even the adamant groups who rejected the refugees were so horrified that they changed their tunes to assuage their guilt. They just couldn't imagine that humans could be so cruel to other humans.

"Pretty bleak, huh? Well, many good, thinking people got around to actually reading the New Testament on their own. The disciples Matthew and Luke defined the essence of Christ's message to mankind. But all too often, the southern preachers... and to some extent northern ones too, would cherry-pick Old Testament homilies and ancient stories, stories that had been greatly edited and modified over the centuries by monks and 'scholars' to define their particular agenda. The King James version of the Bible, for example, is the result of probably three hundred edits from the original Dead Sea Scrolls and other found documents. It bears virtually no resemblance to the Hebrew translation.

"Let's try an experiment on how stories can change. The person at the head of each row will take 3 minutes to write a story of their own making. It doesn't matter what it is. They will read it to the person next to them and that person will tell it to the next person, and so on until it gets told to the last person in the row. That person will then write down what they were told. We will then read the original story and the final version."

It took about a half-hour for this experiment to transact. When the beginning and ending stories were read out loud, they were virtually nothing alike except for a few of the basic facts. Much laughter and shock told Hullaby all he needed to know that this lesson was a success to his points made. "Remember, folks, in Biblical times beginning about 5,000 years ago, there were no smart phones, no internet, no television, and the like. Only the elite 1% were literate, and they usually ran the government or the church/synagogue. You get the idea, don't you?"

Everyone left class muttering about what was true and what was not. Sonya's smart phone rang. It was Derek. "Hi, Sonya. What ya doin'?"

"I'm just getting out of class and heading to the studio to work out. What about you?"

"Oh, I'm getting ready for the weekend, so why don't you pack up your stuff and come visit for a couple days? One of my teammates and his parents are leaving town and told me I could have the house. It's not a big house, but it will be OUR house for a couple days. How's that sound?"

"It sounds great. Where shall I meet you?"

"At the student center. When can I expect you?"

"Well, it's ten-thirty, so if I left at eleven, probably one-thirty or two."

"Great. See you then. I've got something to discuss. Pack your workout clothes and running shoes. See ya."

Now what?

Sonya made the drive wishing she were already there. It was midday on a Friday, so the traffic was a little heavy causing her to arrive a little later than planned. He was waiting on the steps. When he saw her coming, he trotted over to her dangling a keychain. "Let's go. We can pick up a lunch on the way."

They picked up lunch at a local sandwich shop and dashed to Derek's buddy's house. The lunch was put in the refrigerator as the two lovers suddenly realized they had other priorities. After a couple hours of long-awaited lovemaking, they went downstairs and ate their lunches for dinner. There were a couple of cold beers left, so they drank them with the sandwiches.

Derek opened a separate conversation with, "I want you to meet somebody tomorrow that I think will interest you. Did you ever hear of a track and field event called the *heptathlon?*"

"No. What is that?"

"It's an Olympic event that covers seven events. You know, "hepta" is the Latin prefix for seven."

"No, I didn't know that. What are the events?"

"Okay. There's a sprint, long jump, hurdles, high jump, javelin, shot put and 800-meter run as the last leg of the heptathlon. This event is supposed to define the best female athletes in the meet, or in the country or world."

"So, what does this guy want with me? Oh, you think I'm going to audition? I don't know anything about this stuff. Sure, I can run fast, but high jump? Really?"

"Yeah. Well, my idea is to also help get you a scholarship so you can come here and get a degree and, uh, well, be near each other."

"Ah, so that's your big idea. Well, I love you for the thought. But what if I'm not good enough? What then?"

"Well, we'll see about that. You said you wanted to do something good and worthwhile. You also said you were questioning the point of your physical skills and training if all you were doing was teaching old men and women how to escape a choke hold. Let's see what you can do tomorrow."

After a warm, loving and relaxing afternoon, they watched some TV and went to bed early. Next morning, Derek made them a light breakfast after they showered together and went to the school track and field venue. It was tucked in next to the brick field house and locker rooms. There were several athletes already there stretching and jogging, practicing on hurdles and generally getting ready for a full practice this Saturday morning. Derek waved at a short, stocky man with a buzz cut and a stopwatch and whistle around his neck. He was considerably shorter than both Derek and Sonya and peered up at them through squinting blue eyes.

"Stan, this is the woman I told you about, Sonya Keller. Sonya, Stan Hunter. Mr. Hunter is a former national decathlon champion. I told him about you, and he wanted to see for himself."

"Hello, Ms. Keller. Your boyfriend speaks very highly of you. I'm interested in seeing how you can help the Ball State women's track and field team. Are you interested in trying out?"

"Well, nice to meet you too, Mr. Hunter. Since my boyfriend brought me to Muncie under mysterious circumstances, I guess I can't show him up by saying no," she said smiling her most charming smile.

"Call me Stan. Why don't you stretch and do some light jogging to warm up? Then find me and we'll see what we can see," Hunter said before smiling and walking away. Sonya noticed his bulging calf muscles and even though he lacked a chiseled physique, she could see real power in his shoulders and back.

"You should see that guy's office. He's got pictures of himself holding trophies and such. He was built like a rock back in the day. Well, let's get you ready."

They stretched the way Sonya had taught him in preparing for a martial arts event. "No pulled muscles if you please," she said, chidingly, back then. They then jogged a couple of slow laps and ran across the infield to Hunter's location where he was coaching some high jump technique.

"What's first?" Sonya asked. Derek waved and went back to running laps.

"Let's see what kind of foot speed you have. I want you to run one lap as fast as you can. It's 400 meters. Have you ever run that far before?"

Smiling, Sonya said, "Oh sure. Tell me when to start."

"On the whistle." She situated herself on the track and got into a semi-crouch. When Hunter thought she was ready, he blew the whistle and off she went. At halfway down the back stretch he had her at 22 seconds. She finished the other half lap in 27 seconds. Forty-nine flat.

"Pretty good, Sonya. The current school record for 400 meters at Ball State is 52.2. Congratulations. Let's walk over to the shotput cage and see what you can do there."

"I don't know the first thing about doing this. Show me the basics."

Hunter put down his clipboard and showed her how to place the ball next to her chin, speed across the ring backwards, then twisting her torso and extending her arm as quickly as possible in a pushing motion. He told her to be sure to snap the shot off her fingertips at the very end to get a little more velocity on the ball. She tried a couple of unspectacular throws, and he coached her up a bit. "Okay. Let me try on my own."

Sonya's next throw was just over 50 feet. Her second throw went 60 feet. "Very good, Sonya. Now, try to increase your launch angle to get more air under the shot when you throw it."

She tried this and the shot cleared 68 feet. "Well, another school record. Not bad.

Have you ever thrown a javelin?"

"What's that?"

Hunter's laconic responses to her efforts were getting on her nerves a little, but she tried to ignore that. He wasn't being condescending, just being a coach. She knew this technique too.

"Over here." Hunter picked up something that looked like a spear, but without a snell point. There was something wrapped around the spear about in the middle. He showed her the basics of holding it by the wrapped area and getting the javelin launched without it turning sideways in the air. He showed her that there was a run-up to the foul line where she was supposed to launch the javelin. She had some trouble at first, but finally figured out how to launch the spear straight down range without the run up. She just stood still then twisted her torso and tried to launch the javelin in a straight trajectory. Her first measured throw with a run-up went 140 feet. Her second went 166 feet. "Okay. Like with the shot, put some air under it."

She sprinted up to the foul line and launched the javelin an astonishing 198 feet. "Another school record." By this time, everyone was standing around watching this large, powerful woman do things they'd never seen before.

"Sonya, you are a natural athlete the likes of which I've never heard of never mind seen before. I want to see you in two other events and then we'll call it a day. First, go over to that row of starting blocks. I'll teach you how to start from them for a 100-meter trial."

"I've been timed in this before a couple years ago. No blocks, though."

"Fine. Let's see how that works. Hey, Debbie! Do me a favor and start Sonya here. Show her how to use the blocks. Drop your arm when you say go. I'll go down here for timing."

The woman athlete showed Sonya the starting positions for the three commands emphasizing that holding still at "set" was really important. She then gave Sonya the "ready, set, go" commands and dropped her arm. Sonya exploded out of the blocks and hit top speed in five strides. She shot past Hunter where he could feel the breeze she created. "Ten point seven, Sonya. I may have messed up. Can you do this again? Walk back, get your breath and let's see if I can do it right."

The next dash he timed in 10.68. Ridiculous. "My dear girl, you are just a couple tenths of a second off the world record for women. Amazing. Where have you been? Let's see how you do in the 800, now that I've tired you out some."

"I FEEL GOOD. I WORK out a lot. I run maybe 7 or 8 miles a day. Let me stretch a little." She stretched, got her breath and came over to where Hunter was waiting.

"Ready? Set, go!"

Sonya's running form was like watching ballet. She seemed to float around the track. The athletes watching started cheering her on. She zoomed past Hunter in 58 seconds. Sensing that they were seeing something special, everyone continued their yelling and cheering. With 200 meters left, Sonya started straining, but didn't lose her form. One minute, 58 seconds! "Another school record. Put on your sweats, cool down and come to my office, please." Hunter waved at Derek to follow him.

"Where did you find this woman, Derek? She just set four school records. I don't even have to watch her long jump."

"I first saw her playing basketball in a pick-up game. She proceeded to do a two-hand dunk over my pals. You should see her do *karate*. She's like lightning. I took her to a batting cage, and in 10 minutes she was pounding everything into the net. I saw her throw a baseball 250 feet on a line. That's why I thought of you and her. Do you think you could coach her up to participate in heptathlon?"

"I can't wait to try. Here she comes. Sonya! Let's go into my office."

When they arrived at Hunter's office, he sat down and pulled out some forms. "Sonya, this is an offer sheet for a full athletic scholarship for track and field. I'd like you to begin in the summer session and even start some classes. I've never seen anyone like you before, and I think your potential as a world-class track and field athlete is unlimited. NOBODY throws a javelin 190 feet on their first try at it. You did that. Your track speed is astonishing. I would love to have you as part of the Ball State University track and field organization. How old are you?"

"I'm twenty-two. I'll be twenty-three in the fall. Aren't I a little old to be starting college?"

"Don't worry about that. A person is never too old to start or finish college. What do you say? Do you want to be part of our program and, incidentally, get a first-class education too?"

Sonya looked at Derek and saw him smiling broadly. "Let me have my phone, baby," she said to him. She dialed up her mother. "Mom! I'm in Muncie. Yeah. I'm sitting in a coach's office at Ball State. He wants to offer me a full scholarship to run track and field. Do you think I should sign up?"

The screech from the phone was loud enough to be heard by everyone. Sonya held the phone away from her head to let the men hear her mother's obvious joy. "So, I take that as a yes. Yeah. Who knew? I'll be home tomorrow and fill you in on the details. Bye.

"Well, Mr. Hunter, I guess that settles it. Where do I sign?"

"Derek, make sure you send her all the application paperwork she needs to fill out. I'll do what I have to do from this end. Sonya, you'll have to fill out the application and all that paperwork that includes your transcripts and stuff. This is late April, so I'd like you to get this going right away so we can have you down here in June when summer classes start. I'll do whatever I can to make the transition easy for you."

As Sonya and Derek left the coach's office and walked back across the track and infield, they were stopped by several of the athletes, both men and women. They asked her if she was coming to school there and how did she get so fast and strong. Sonya was more than a little flabbergasted at the attention and questions but tried to be polite in answering.

Later, as she and Derek drove back to the house, she asked, "But where will we, er, I, live?"

"I liked the 'we' part. That's gonna be a discussion for another time when we don't have anything else distracting us. That decision has all sorts of implications, so we better have clear heads. On another subject... What do you think you want to study?"

"Well, since I seem to have some experience with the subject, maybe criminal justice. I'm known, in some circles as the *Angel of Justice*, you know."

Sonya had to pull over to the curb while they both laughed themselves into folded up heaps. When they finally gathered themselves, she looked at him and her tears started to flow. "Is this what those philosophers meant when they said that good things will happen to the righteous?" she said.

"I think so, darling. And you are gonna have nothing but good things from now on. I love you and want to be part of your happiness."

"I can't tell you how often I've thought about hearing those words or feeling that they have a really good chance at coming true," she said. "So, how long do you think it will take me to throw that damned spear more than 200 feet?"

Acknowledgements

THIS AND SUBSEQUENT PROJECTS WERE written by me, of course, but without the inputs, support and encouragement from my loving spouse, Elaine, I probably would have stopped trying to get published. But the echoes of my maternal grandfather, Mikhail Pastok, a Ukrainian immigrant, kept pushing me to never quit anything that I felt was worthy. And so, Grandpa, here we are.

My beta readers and editors who also kept my literary fires burning include Ms. Belinda Micciulli Martin, my friend and former student, Ms. Jody Kerr who copy edited this manuscript thus creating the need for yet another content edit. Molly Wingate kept encouraging me over the last several years to keep at it with little comments like, "So what else are you doing with yourself?" Ms. Sally Kling, my longest-known friend and confidant stepped away from our friendship enough to also give encouragement and content advice.

With this being my first novel, I have to extend my thanks and appreciation to Mr. Arnold Hamilton of *The Oklahoma Observer* for his continued support with my non-fiction books and printing my op-ed columns in his newspaper.

In case it wasn't all that obvious, I must dedicate this effort to my late mother, Sophie "Sasha" Turner. She was my rock when she was alive and remains a force in my life even today.

About the Author

VERNON TURNER IS THE AUTHOR of five non-fiction books on politics and public education. Meadows and Minefields is his first novel. Now, The Ten Arms of Durga joins the list of fiction and non-fiction books written by Vernon. He wrote a weekly op-ed column for five years at the award-winning River Cities Daily Tribune in Marble Falls, TX and his columns still appear regularly in The Oklahoma Observer. In previous careers, he wrote many biological and manufacturing engineering articles for scientific and trade journals.

Vernon draws on a wealth of experience as a world traveler, a scientist, an educator and an engineer in various industries while living in six states, the latest being Colorado. He is a devoted researcher as his science/engineering professions required. He earned a Bachelor of Science degree in Zoology and Chemistry from Ohio University and a Master of Science degree in Biology from San Diego State University. His teaching career spans the breadth of teaching anatomy as a graduate assistant at SDSU and as an anatomy laboratory instructor at Wright State University Medical School. During his six years as a combat medical specialist in the U.S. Army/National Guard, Vernon taught combat first-aid to incoming trainees. Vernon's most recent teaching career centered around teaching

Language Arts and all sciences in grades 6-12 in public schools in Colorado and Texas. These years included teaching Advanced Placement Physics and AP Biology.

Vernon's world travels include the United Kingdom/Scotland, Mexico, Canada, Greenland, Uganda, Tanzania (where he climbed Mt. Kilimanjaro), China, New Zealand and the Galapagos Islands in Ecuador.

Vernon loves sports – even played several in his day – and tries to stay fit and remain sharp of wit. He regularly thanks his former students for aiding in that action. He now lives happily with his spouse of thirty years in Denver, Colorado where he is happily owned by two spectacular Maine Coon cats.

Lightning Source UK Ltd.
Milton Keynes UK
UKHW010935100720
366326UK00001B/261